Missing

Mike Paull

A Wings ePress, Inc.
Spy Thriller

Wings ePress, Inc.

Edited by: Jeanne Smith
Copy Edited by: Brian Hatfield
Executive Editor: Jeanne Smith
Cover Artist: Trisha FitzGerald-Jung
Photo 71719374 ©Angelo Cordeschi|Dreamstime.com

Wings ePress Books
www.wingsepress.com

Copyright © 2021 by: Mike Paull
ISBN-13: 978-1-61309-544-7

Published In the United States Of America

Wings ePress Inc.
3000 N. Rock Road
Newton, KS 67114

What They Are Saying About

Missing

Retired dentist and licensed pilot Mike Paull has crafted an international spy thriller. It takes readers to a post-Saddam Iraq where a small group of Americans from "the Agency" want to track down the rumored stash of gold Saddam hid away before his execution. The mission results in Craig Cooper being shot in the back. A flawed family man, Coop recovers and is sucked back into the now-revived mission, along with ally Zoe Fields, who find their lives threatened as they unravel the mystery and confront traitors in their midst. The stakes are high, the action never stops, and Paull knows precisely how to keep the pages turning until the very end.

—Dan Barnett, book columnist, Chico (CA) Enterprise-Record

The title of this taut, compelling mystery is paradoxical. The story features something that's gone missing but there is no element of a good mystery that is missing in Paull's book. Paull's characters are believable, the double-dealing that makes the plot suspenseful is subtle, and, thankfully, Paull avoids cliches. His treatment of "the agency" (read CIA) rings true, given what we know of how the dark side of our foreign policy operates. Rules are ignored, personal relationships are forsaken when the mission or ambition requires it, people are expendable. In less able hands, this could be a horror story but Paull's deft touch reveals a redemptive core of honor and bravery. The result is a very satisfying read."

—Jan E. Dizard, Professor Emeritus, Amherst College

I am still breathing deeply after finishing the book. I LOVED it... the characters were interesting and well-drawn, and the twists and turns were compelling and exciting. GOOD JOB!

—C. K. Griswold, freelance mystery editor

My Thanks

I would like to thank Nora Profit, founder of the Writing Loft. Her coaching transformed a journeyman writer into a true storyteller.

I would also like to thank my beta readers: Scott Paulo, Jan Dizard, Robin Dizard and Tom Lear. They had the courage to critique a friend's story and the insight to provide detailed feedback on plot, characters, clarity and pacing.

My thanks to the Wings ePress, Inc. CEO, Linda Voth, who found the story intriguing and passed it on to her executive editor. And my special thanks to Executive Editor Jeanne Smith. She guided me through the Wings' process with the knowledge and ease of a true professional.

Last but not least, thanks to my loving wife, Bev, who over the last several years has graciously responded to the same question over and over again: "How does this sound?"

Dedication

To my beautiful wife Bev. My greatest critic
and my greatest fan.

* * *

"There is no knife that cuts so sharply and with such poisoned blade as treachery."

—Ouida

One

Baghdad, Iraq... December 30, 2006

His ankles were shackled, and he strained against the noose that chafed the sides of his neck. His wrists were bound, but he managed to cradle a copy of the Quran. He read aloud to make his voice heard above the shouting and he spewed back curses that were hurled at him. Today, Saddam Hussein, the man who built the scaffold and condemned so many to it, would himself die on it.

The Americans agreed the execution would be handled by the Iraqis. That meant no U.S. military; however, two Americans were allowed to attend: Randy Nichols, the station chief for the American Intelligence unit in Baghdad, and his partner, Craig Cooper.

As the big moment drew closer, the mood of the onlookers morphed from anger to rage and finally to hysteria. A glassy-eyed man dressed in a loosely-fitting robe and a wrapped head scarf, maneuvered for a more advantageous position. He wedged his shoulders between Coop and Randy and when he was in range, he delivered the ultimate insult in this part of the world. He slipped off his sandals and one at a time launched them at Saddam.

The executioner pulled a hood from his pocket and tried to place it over Saddam's head. Saddam jerked away and spit on the man's shirt. The hangman shrugged and looked to the group of military officers seated in the front row. The one with the thickest mustache and the largest cluster of medals nodded. The executioner tugged on a handle and the floor dropped from under Saddam. The sound of his neck snapping, like a dead branch being ripped from a giant oak, temporarily muted the apoplectic spectators.

Witnessing a man die wasn't new to Coop, and he was trained not to have a visceral response, but this time he could taste the bile from his stomach rise to the bottom of his throat. He swallowed hard to force it back and he peered around the room; the delirium was starting all over again. He spotted the door and headed for it.

He let the door slam behind him. The quiet of the hallway was a welcome relief. He leaned against the wall and lit a cigarette, but before he could get a second drag, the door opened and Randy stepped out to join him. "You left in a hurry," he said.

Coop inhaled, savoring the bitter taste of the unfiltered Turkish tobacco before letting the smoke seep out through his nostrils. "Yeah, I ran out of popcorn."

Randy squinted and shook his head. "I don't get it. What's your problem?"

"I just don't think a hanging should be a spectator sport."

"Look, the asshole's dead. That's all that matters. Who knows, maybe it'll make our job easier."

"Maybe." Coop tossed his cigarette to the concrete floor, but before he could snuff it out, the door opened and throngs of people spilled into the hallway. The crowd moved toward the exit, sweeping Coop and Randy along in the wave.

The Camp Justice military base had cordoned off a section of the parade grounds nearest the prison and turned it into a parking lot for the day's spectacle. As Coop and Randy approached, a wind off the Tigris River blew a damp mist through the air that permeated Coop's windbreaker. He began to shiver and hugged his shoulders. Randy keyed the lock to their mud-spattered Honda and settled in behind the wheel. Coop lost no time slipping into the seat next to him.

Two soldiers waved the line of cars through the gates and onto the road bordering the river. Coop looked at his watch. It wasn't yet 7 a.m., but in spite of the dank weather, the streets were jammed with civilians. They were laughing and cheering, some were dancing and a few were even firing guns into the air.

"Okay, he's dead. So, how d'ya figure it'll be easier for us now?" Coop said.

"I'm thinking it may loosen up some tongues. I've got a guy who wants to meet with us tonight."

"A guy? What guy?"

"I'm not sure, but he says he knows where Saddam hid the gold."

Coop suppressed a laugh, holding it to a smirk. "That's convenient. Where did he come from all of a sudden?"

"Probably heard about the reward."

"So did the last dozen guys. You know how that turned out."

Randy shook his head. "Don't be such a fuckin' cynic, it's the way our job works, right?"

The question sounded rhetorical; Coop ignored it. Instead, he lit another cigarette. Randy narrowed his eyes and shot him an icy look. It was the same one Coop's mother planted on him when he was thirteen and she caught him in the basement smoking one of his dad's cigars.

Coop opened his window and fanned the smoke in its direction as he surveyed the landscape. He was told Baghdad was once a beautiful city, but that was before the invasion of 2003 and well before he arrived thirteen months ago. Now it was pretty grim. Boarded-up buildings were covered with graffiti, homeless camps dotted the roadway, and a stench from the polluted Tigris river overpowered the fresh fragrance of the morning drizzle.

One section of the city, the International Green Zone, hadn't changed. It still looked as it did before the war. Thick concrete walls and heavily armed guards surrounded Saddam's former presidential complex. Within its walls, thousands of Americans, mostly government employees, lived and worked and played. They referred to it as the Ultimate Gated Community.

Randy pulled to the West Gate where two Humvees and a half dozen soldiers were strategically positioned next to the entrance. One of the soldiers, sporting sergeant stripes on his sleeve, approached the driver's side of the Honda. "Morning, sir. Credentials?"

Coop handed his papers to Randy, who piled his own on top and passed them to the sergeant. The guard examined the documents, handed them back to Randy and signaled another soldier to open the barrier.

"Have a good day, sir," the sergeant said. Randy gave an artificial salute and drove into the Green Zone.

"So, what time are we meeting this guy?" Coop asked.

"Around midnight."

Coop stared at him. "He can't get into the Green Zone that late at night."

"He won't have to. The meeting's in Sadr City."

The hair on the back of Coop's neck stood on end. "You're kidding me. That's the body bag capital of Iraq."

"That's where he wants to meet, okay? So don't worry about it."

"Doesn't smell right to me."

Randy pulled into the Embassy garage and squeezed the Honda between a couple of SUVs. "It doesn't matter. You're not going."

"What're you saying?"

"I'm saying you've got a crappy attitude. I'll handle it myself."

"Bullshit, you're not going to Sadr City alone."

"Ahmad will be with me."

"He's an interpreter. He doesn't even carry a weapon. I'm going with you."

"No, you're not."

Coop's face turned crimson and his eyes narrowed. "So, you're asking me to stay home?"

Randy got out of the car and slammed the door as hard as he could. "It's not a request, it's an order."

Two

Ahmad was young for his job—only twenty-three—but he had a couple of things going for him. He was born in Baghdad, knew it like the back of his hand and he spoke English so flawlessly he was often taken for a Brit. He was the perfect fit to multitask as driver and interpreter.

The choice from the motor pool was an Opel or a Ford. The temperature had dropped another twelve degrees, so Ahmad picked the Ford. It had the better heater. Randy arrived just before eleven-fifteen and slipped into the passenger seat. Despite the cold temperature, beads of sweat dotted his forehead. His left eye began to twitch, a sign his nagging habit had returned. He handed Ahmad a piece of paper. "Can you find it?"

He studied the Sadr City address. "It's not a problem, but you know this area is crawling with insurgents, and Americans aren't safe there."

A voice from the back seat piped up. "That's why I'm coming along."

Randy turned around and saw Coop grinning like a Cheshire cat. "Damn it, Coop. Get outa the car."

"No."

"I'm still in charge around here. I said, get out."

Coop lit a cigarette and settled back into the seat. Ahmad grimaced. He'd been witness to other arguments between these two. "Sir, we're going to be late," he said.

Randy checked his watch. "Shit. Okay, get going." He glared at Coop. "When we get back, you can pack your bags."

A threat from Randy was not something new. Coop knew if the meeting went well and history repeated itself, Randy would renege and forget all about tonight. They'd be laughing over it at breakfast tomorrow morning.

Ahmad stopped at the exit gate and rolled down his window. The night sergeant peered in and asked if they'd be returning tonight. Ahmad turned to Randy who leaned toward the open window. "Yeah, we'll be back in a couple of hours." The sergeant signaled for the gate to open.

They drove out of the gate and onto the nearby boulevard. It was crowded for this time of night, but a couple of miles to the east the four lanes shrank to two and the traffic thinned. Five minutes later, the Ford was the only car on the road. Ahmad spotted an unlit alley and took a quick left into the pitch-black hole. He pulled to a stop in front of a set of run-down buildings that appeared to be one step ahead of a bulldozer. He cut the lights.

They'd been through this drill before—a couple minutes of wait time before their eyes accommodated to the darkness. The details of the buildings began to come into focus. Randy and Coop unholstered their pistols and the three men got out of the car. About twenty yards ahead, they spied the glow of a cigarette and inched toward it. Randy poked Ahmad's shoulder. "His name's Mustafa."

Ahmad shouted in the direction of the light. "Mustafa?"

A bearded man dressed in peasant clothing came into view. He was trembling and barely able to hold his cigarette. His eyes darted around the perimeter. He said something in Arabic. Randy leaned toward Ahmad, "Ask him what he has for us."

Ahmad rattled off a few words in Arabic and waited for a response. "He says he has the information you're looking for, but he wants to know about the reward first."

"That figures. Tell him it depends on the info."

"He says he knows where Saddam hid the gold."

"How could he know that?" Coop asked.

Arabic got thrown back and forth between Ahmad and Mustafa, while Randy and Coop stood by. Ahmad turned to Randy. "He says he grew up with Saddam in Tikrit. He helped him when he was on the run."

Coop said, "So wh..."

Randy held up his hand. "Coop, I'll handle this. Okay?"

Coop pursed his lips and clenched his teeth. "Yeah. Fine."

"Tell him I could care less who helped Saddam. Ask him about the gold," Randy said.

"He says he was with Saddam when several trucks unloaded a bunch of barrels into a warehouse. There were armed guards all over the place."

"So why did he think it was gold?"

"Because Saddam said it was," Ahmad answered.

"Okay. Tomorrow he takes us to the warehouse."

Mustafa muttered a few sentences to Ahmad. Ahmad looked at Randy. "He wants to know how much first."

"Tell him twenty-thousand American...but only if the gold's there."

Ahmad passed the number to Mustafa, who mumbled a few words back to him. "He wants something more. He wants you to get him and his family out of the country."

Randy shook his head. "That wasn't part of the deal."

"He knows that, but he says as soon as Saddam went to the gallows, his life was put in danger. He says you're not the only one who will come looking for the gold."

Coop leaned over to whisper into Randy's ear, but Randy waved him off and said to Ahmad, "Okay, if the gold's in the warehouse, we'll get them to Turkey." He pulled a wad of bills from his pocket and handed it to Mustafa. "Five thousand...the rest depends on what we find in the warehouse."

Mustafa grasped the cash. Out of the darkness, a red laser dot appeared on his neck. Coop recognized it immediately and lunged to push Mustafa out of the way, but a flash and a simultaneous gunshot burst from an adjacent building. Reflexively, Mustafa's left hand reached for his neck where blood spurted from the wound. He crumpled to the ground with his right hand still clutching the money.

"Goddammit, goddammit, get to the car," Randy yelled. Coop and Ahmad took off, but Randy paused to pry the money from the dead man's grip.

Ahmad, the youngest and the fastest of the group, reached the car first and jumped into the driver's seat. Coop was only a few steps behind. Randy, who was carrying an extra layer of fat around his midsection, was not able to keep up and lagged several yards back.

Another gunshot rang out. Coop kept running, but after a few strides felt a hot sensation working its way down his back. He reached around to tug at his shirt; it was wet and sticky. The heat intensified until it felt like a hot poker was working its way into his lungs. He dropped to his knees, looked at his blood-soaked hand and fell face down in the dirt.

He wasn't sure how long he lay there, but when he regained consciousness, his nostrils were filled with the sweet smell of charcoal with a hint of sulfur—the unmistakable odor of gunpowder. He knew he had to get to the car, but his legs felt like jelly, so he crawled. He clawed at the dirt and he pulled himself forward, an inch at a time until he sensed he was close. He strained to lift his head and blinked several times as he peered into the darkness. The car was gone.

Three

Washington, D.C.—September 13, 2007

It had been a restless night for Coop. After tossing and turning for the last few hours, he grabbed his phone from the nightstand. It read 4:47 a.m. Quietly, so as not to wake Fran, he slipped out of bed. He glanced back. His wife was still sound asleep.

Coop stepped into the bathroom, closed the door and turned on the lights. There were mirrors on both walls and he could see the reflection of his back. The harsh ceiling light made the lump of scar tissue glisten as if it had just been waxed and polished. He splashed cold water on his face, pulled on a pair of boxers and flipped off the overhead.

The Cooper house was a typical Arlington Virginia two-story—living room, dining room and kitchen on the main floor and three bedrooms on the top level. Coop and Fran had the master, their ten-year-old son Josh occupied the one adjacent and Coop had converted the small one down the hall into an office.

He went into the office and closed the door. The desk was shoved into a corner to create space for two large corkboards resting on easels. The corkboards were overflowing with dozens of notes.

Coop removed the pins and notes and began rearranging them for what seemed like the hundredth time. He placed SADDAM EXECUTED above MIDNIGHT MEETING and placed INFORMANT ASSASSINATED below OPERATION SUSPENDED. He put COOP SHOT to the right of SNIPER and then, when he could feel his pulse throbbing in the front of his forehead, he pulled them out and flung them against the wall.

"When are you going to give it up?" a voice from behind said.

Coop turned to see Fran standing in the doorway. Although every week he promised her he'd let it go, it had been all he could think about since he'd left the hospital. Every day for the last nine months, over and over again, he rehashed the events of his shooting. This time he said, "I think I've found a connection."

Fran gazed at the pins and notes strewn across the floor. "That's not a connection, it's a mess."

He looked down at the notes. There was something about the way they lay next to each other that suggested an idea Coop hadn't considered. "I just thought of a new theory. What if..."

Fran stared at him with a look that blended anger with pity. "I don't want to hear it."

"But look, there might be something here."

"You don't see it, do you?

"See what?'

"What this is doing to you...to me...to Josh."

Coop was silent. He knelt and began separating the pins from the notes. "Just give me a couple more weeks. I prom..."

Fran did an about-face and stomped out of the room. Coop ran after her and managed to grab her arm before she reached the bedroom. "Fran...a week. Just one more week."

She yanked her arm from his grasp. "Our family can't wait a week. Oh God, you're eating us up. You're consuming us."

Coop felt his stomach twist into a knot. He looked down at his left hand; it was still clutching the notes. Fran picked up a wastebasket and held it in front of him. "Throw that crap away and use your energy to reconnect with your son. He misses you."

"What's wrong with me?" Coop bit at his lower lip and emptied the notes into the basket. I...I want to be a good husband...a good father, but I...I can't stop thinking about that night. I'm so sorry..."

Fran stopped him in the middle of his sentence. "Don't apologize, just do it. I'll help you. We'll beat this, but you have to commit."

"I will. I'll commit. I'll beat it." He hugged Fran and she hugged him back. Coop gave her a kiss and went into the bedroom to get ready for the day ahead.

He hadn't seen a real assignment since Iraq; most of his days were spent in front of a computer doing research for someone else. His usual wardrobe was a pair of khakis and a polo, but today he took one of his two white shirts from the drawer, plucked his only tie from the rack and grabbed his blue blazer from the closet.

Coop hung the jacket over a kitchen chair. By force of habit, he turned on the coffee machine and tapped a button on the TV remote. He took out a cigarette. Every day he told himself this was the day he would quit. He put it back in the pack.

The machine beeped. Coop filled a mug and worked on the black coffee while he split his attention between the morning paper and the channel 4 news. The screen caught his attention. A picture of an Airbus 320 appeared and the newscaster was blabbering. "...still no signs of Burma Airlines flight five-seven-one. The last contact with the plane was over the Indian Ocean five days ago..."

Josh strolled into the kitchen. His golden retriever Rusty, as usual, was clinging to him like a shadow. Coop muted the TV. "Hey, buddy, you're up early."

"Hi, Dad. Any OJ?"

"Yeah, sure, bottom shelf." Coop pointed to the fridge.

Josh poured himself a glass of juice and dropped a frozen waffle into the toaster. He sat facing Coop. "Why are you wearing a tie?"

"Oh, I've got a meeting with the deputy director this afternoon."

Josh forced down a sip of juice. "Do...do you have to?"

"Yeah, I do. You know that."

Josh pushed the juice away. "Dad, are they going to make you go away again?"

"No buddy, don't worry. I'm not going anywhere."

Tears welled in Josh's eyes. The toaster popped. He stood, retrieved his waffle and smeared it with a wad of butter and a spoonful of jam. On his way back to the table, the waffle slid off the plate and landed jam-side down on the floor. Josh stared at it. His lip began to quiver and his chest began to heave.

Coop jumped up and put his arms around Josh, who was crying hysterically.

"Hey, it's okay. It's just a waffle." He patted Josh's back. "Look, I'm not going anywhere and I'm not going to get hurt."

Josh gained control and wiped his tears with the cuff of his shirt. "Promise?"

"Promise," Coop said.

Fran entered the kitchen. She was dressed in hospital scrubs with the nameplate—F. Cooper RN—pinned to her top. "Promise what?" she said.

"Dad promised he's not going away again."

Fran looked at Coop, but answered Josh. "That's great. Great news." She stared down at the mess on the floor.

"Oh, just an accident. I'll clean it up," Coop said. He peeked at his watch. "Josh, get ready for school. I'll make you a waffle to go."

Josh started for the stairs. Rusty's ears perked and he trotted out to join him. Coop put another waffle in the toaster and Fran poured herself a cup of coffee. "You have to stand by it this time. He's afraid you'll get shot again," she said.

Coop looked away. "I know."

Fran pushed back from the table and went to Coop. She turned his head to make eye contact. "You have to stand by it. He's counting on you."

"You heard...I gave him my promise."

Fran went back to her coffee. "I'm scrubbing in today. Can you drop Josh off?

"Yeah, no problem."

"Are you sure? You have that meeting."

"It's not 'til this afternoon."

Josh returned to the kitchen wearing a raincoat with a backpack slung over one shoulder. "You ready, Dad? I only have fifteen minutes."

He grabbed his coat and handed Josh the waffle, then looked down at the spill.

"I'll clean it up," Fran said. She gave Josh a kiss on the forehead and Coop a peck on the cheek. "Get going." Before they reached the door, she shouted to Coop, "By the way, did you go in for those follow-up X-rays on your lung?"

"Yeah, I went in yesterday. See ya tonight." He nudged Josh out the door and closed it behind him.

Coop maneuvered his Chevy as close as he could to the front of the school and wedged in behind an SUV that was unloading a carpool of kids. Josh grabbed his backpack and opened the passenger door. "You better run for it. It's starting to rain," Coop said. Josh got out and started to close the door.

Coop leaned over. "Hey, how 'bout a kiss?" Josh scanned the schoolyard for onlookers. He leaned over and kissed Coop on the cheek.

"Don't forget, we're going to the basketball game tonight," Coop said.

"I can't wait." Josh waved and dashed toward the front door.

Four

Randy couldn't have been more pleased. A promotion from a station chief to deputy director of the Agency was a leap not often made in this tight-knit bureaucracy. To fit with his new position, he made changes to his persona, starting with his wardrobe. When he returned from Iraq, he didn't have a suit to his name. Today he was dressed to the nines in a three-piece, blue pinstripe with a red tie.

Director Dutton rarely summoned a deputy to his office; Randy could feel the butterflies. When the receptionist called him yesterday, she had said: "nine o'clock sharp." Randy looked at his watch. He was ten minutes early. He took a seat and opened a technical journal that might as well have been written in Greek. He feigned interest.

The receptionist announced that the director was ready to see him. Randy tossed the magazine back on the table and followed her into the office. Two oversized flags flanked the desk and the walls were covered with dozens of framed photos showing the director with celebrities, congressmen, and even the president.

Director Dutton was behind his desk talking on the phone. He looked up and waved two fingers in the air, signaling Randy to take a seat facing him. "Well, tell him to fuck himself," Dutton shouted into the phone before he slammed it into its cradle. He looked at Randy. "Have you gotten used to those yet?"

"I'm working on it."

The director leaned back with his hands behind his neck. "So, Randy, have you talked to Cooper yet?"

Randy's left eye twitched and he rubbed it as if a speck of something had gotten into it. "Not yet. He's coming in this afternoon."

"Good, get him on board and get this thing going."

Randy shifted in his chair and rubbed his eye again. Dutton glanced at his watch. "Well? What is it?"

"Sir, I'm thinking of sending Torelli instead."

"Torelli? Who the fuck's Torelli?"

"Marco Torelli. He's one of our up-and-coming stars."

"Never heard of him. How long's he been with the Agency?'

"A couple of years."

"A couple of years doesn't mean shit in this business. You know that. Forget him. Send Cooper."

"I was thinking this would be a good experience for him."

"Let him get experience somewhere else. I want Cooper."

"Sir, you may not know it, but Coop's head is screwed up."

"Says who?"

"I found out he's been seeing a shrink."

"So what? Every guy who gets shot sees a shrink."

"I know, but something...something's not right with this guy."

The director stood. "Look, Randy, Cooper knows what he's doing and I like him. I considered him for this job, but I went with you instead. Don't make me think it was a mistake."

"It wasn't a mistake, sir. Cooper will be on board this afternoon."

"Good. Say hello to him for me."

Five

The rain was heavy and the wind was howling when Coop parked his Chevy in the government building lot. An umbrella was useless; the rain stabbed at his face like little slivers of glass. He pulled his trench coat over his head and sprinted toward the entrance.

The lobby looked like all D.C. buildings have looked since 9-11. The marble vestibule was bisected by a plexiglass partition fitted with a security entrance and a spit-shined Marine wearing a single-ear headset was stationed on the other side of the glass.

Coop shook the water from his soggy coat and approached the partition. He slid his credentials through the slot and talked into the microphone. "Craig Cooper, I have an appointment with the deputy director."

The Marine went through his ritual. He studied the photo on the ID and looked up at Coop's drenched face. "Pretty nasty out there?"

"Nasty? That would be an improvement."

The Marine laughed. "Are you carrying a weapon, sir?"

"Yeah, a Glock 23."

The Marine slid a pouch through the slot. "You know the drill. You can pick it up on your way out."

Coop lifted his pistol from its holster and dropped it into the pouch. The Marine exchanged it for Coop's credentials and a day-pass Coop clipped to his lapel. The door buzzed and popped ajar. "Elevator's straight ahead...office is on the top floor. Have a good day, sir," the Marine said.

Coop passed through the entry. "Men's room?"

"Yes, sir. On your left."

Coop peeled off his raincoat and pulled a handful of paper towels from the dispenser. He looked in the mirror as he dried his face. He wasn't happy with the reflection. Gray was sneaking into his sideburns and crow's feet were forming near the corners of his eyes. He checked his watch and clenched his teeth. "Nine months. What're another five minutes?" He put a cigarette between his lips, but before he could light it, the door sprung open and a guy rushed past him, making a beeline for one of the stalls. Coop tossed the cigarette into the trash, grabbed his coat and hustled out.

The reception room was filled with elevator music, *People* magazines, and an attractive secretary. It reminded Coop of a doctor's office, only without the coughing and sneezing. The secretary looked up from her computer. "Mr. Cooper?"

"Yes, ma'am."

"He's expecting you. It shouldn't be more than a couple of minutes, "she said before stepping into the inner office.

Coop stared at the brass plaque on the door as it closed behind her—*Randy Nichols, Deputy Director*. He swallowed hard. "Get used to it," he mumbled to himself.

The door opened and the secretary signaled Coop to go in.

He looked around Randy's office. The desk was cherrywood, the chairs were leather and the picture window overlooked Washington D.C. It was a far cry from the cubby hole Randy used at the embassy in Baghdad. He sprung from his chair and threw his arms around Coop. "Man, it's good to see you."

Coop flashed on the days when he and Randy would greet with a good old bear hug, but today wasn't one of them. He pulled away. "Why am I here?"

"That's it? After all we've been through together?"

"Together? Really?"

"Come on, Coop. We were like brothers out there."

"I don't think a brother would leave a brother face down in the dirt."

Randy ignored the remark and motioned Coop to a leather chair, then he checked his fully-stocked wet bar and selected a bottle. "Black Label okay?"

"Doesn't matter. I'm not here for a social visit."

Randy splashed the Scotch into a couple of glasses. He handed one to Coop and took the seat next to him. They sat without speaking, sipping the liquor. Randy was the first to drain his glass. "Look, Coop, I thought you were dead. I had to make a tough call."

"Did you think I was dead when I was in the hospital? Hell, I've been working in the building next door for the last six months. Where have you been?"

"Listen, I understand you're pissed. I should've come by. I wanted to, but I thought you needed some space. You know, a little time. So..."

"So, bullshit. Why am I here?"

Randy ignored the insult. "Director Dutton wanted you here. He's re-opening the Iraqi Gold Operation."

"What the hell for?"

"What d'ya mean, what the hell for? He wants to find that gold."

"It's been almost ten months. Why me?"

"You're the only one who knew about that operation."

"Well, somebody else must have known or I wouldn't be missing part of a lung."

"Okay, I get that, but shit happens in this job and we don't always know why."

Coop hadn't had a cigarette all day. He took a pack from his pocket and held it up. Randy didn't object and handed him an ashtray. Coop took a deep drag, closed his eyes and leaned back into the soft leather. The memories came back again. Beads of sweat broke out on his forehead.

Randy broke the silence. "Listen, Coop, personally I don't give a damn. The gold's long gone by now, but Dutton's on my ass."

"Well, I'm not your guy."

"Look, I don't expect you to really find the stuff, just give me something to prove to the man upstairs that it's gone."

"I can't do it. I need to be around. I promised my boy."

"Hey, I don't have a big budget for this. You'll only be gone a week...ten days tops." Randy reached over to his desk, picked up a folder labeled SECRET//NOFORN and dropped it into Coop's lap. "At least take a look." Coop ignored the folder. "Go ahead, it won't kill you to give it look," Randy said.

Coop tapped his fingers on the cover. Like his smoking habit, he was able to hold temptation at bay for only so long before it got the best of him. He opened the folder and leafed through a couple of pages. He pulled out a single sheet and held it up. "Are you kidding me? This has only one sentence about me getting shot." Randy didn't respond. Coop closed the folder. "Doesn't matter, I'm not in."

"Well, just think about this for a minute. We can all come out big winners here. The Director will be satisfied that we gave it a shot. I'll be happy to put a final lid on the case and you may get enough closure to sleep at night."

Coop whispered under his breath, "closure." He tossed the folder back to Randy. "I promised my family. I can't do it."

"I'll give you permission to look for your shooter."

"I don't need your goddamn permission."

"I'm just saying...this is your only chance to find him."

Coop ignored Randy, meandered over to the bar, and poured himself another drink. He swallowed it in one gulp, then hurled the empty glass against the wall, spraying shards all over the plush-pile carpet. "Pass that fuckin' folder back to me." Randy held back a grin and slipped it in front of Coop.

He opened the folder and paced back and forth as he read through the pages. Like an addict's fix, he felt euphoria as a shot of adrenalin pumped into his blood stream. "I don't want you looking over my shoulder."

"You'll be in charge."

"How much money do I have?"

"I told you, enough for a week or two."

"I want total access to the embassy's files and databases."

"Not a problem."

"And Billings has to stay the hell outa my way."

"Don't worry, I'll take care of him."

Coop tucked the folder under his arm and started for the door. He stopped and turned. "Oh, and one more thing. I want Zoe Fields to go with me."

Six

Fran was still in her hospital scrubs emptying the dishwasher when Coop walked into the kitchen. "Oh, I didn't hear you come in," she said.

"Yeah, I parked on the street. How did the surgery go?"

"Poor guy lost his pancreas. The surgeon had to tell him he's a diabetic now. How did your meeting go?"

Coop opened the fridge and lifted a beer from the bottom shelf. "Any crackers or nibbles?"

Fran opened a cabinet, took out a bag of chips and tossed them onto the counter. "Well?

Coop was having trouble opening the bag and tore the edge of the package with his front teeth. "Well, what?"

"Your meeting. How did it go?"

"Fine."

"That's it? Fine?"

"Yeah, it went good."

Fran grabbed the chips away from Coop. "You're going back, aren't you?

"Uh...only for a week or two."

Fran turned away, stomped out of the kitchen and slammed the door. A cup bounced off the counter and smashed as it fell into the sink. Coop ran after her, but she closed the bedroom door. He knocked. "Can I come in?" There was no response. He opened the door and went in anyway.

Fran was looking out the window and refused to face him. "How could you? After this morning, how could you?" Coop didn't answer. This time she shouted at the window. "How could you? Answer me."

He inched next to her and put his hand on her shoulder. "Fran, I..."

She shoved his hand away and her voice got louder. "What are you going to tell Josh?" Again, Coop didn't answer. Fran turned toward Coop and yelled. "How are you going to tell him? When?"

Josh's room shared a common wall with the master bedroom. He began bouncing his basketball, harder and faster, until the voices were drowned out.

Coop knocked and poked his head around Josh's door. "Hey, buddy." Josh kept his eyes on the bouncing basketball. "Hey, let's go early to the game. We'll pick up a hot dog for dinner."

Josh still wouldn't make eye contact. "I don't want to go."

"Really? You've been looking forward to this game."

"I changed my mind."

"Hey, the Wizards are in first place."

"I don't care."

"Come on. It'll be fun."

"You promised."

Coop put his arms around Josh and gave him a big hug. "I know it's hard...real hard to understand right now. But..."

Josh pushed him away. "You promised. I understand that."

Seven

There was only one private office in the Agency annex and Coop had it. It was a reward for taking a bullet in the back—the Agency's version of the Purple Heart. He insisted he didn't deserve it, but when it was offered, he didn't turn it down. Coop thumbed through the classified folder. It brought back memories of his thirteen months in Baghdad—some good, some bad, some very bad. A light tap on his door snapped him out of his melancholy. "Come on in."

The door swung open, but before anyone entered, Coop closed his eyes and inhaled deeply through his nostrils and smiled. "I know that perfume," he said aloud.

A head peeked around the corner, "Hey, boss. It's been a while."

Zoe was his favorite. They were almost the same age, but no one would have guessed. She had the angelic look of a college-girl, but underneath it she was as tough as nails. When asked about her disarming persona, Coop would say "she's an angel with a great left hook." They had met fifteen years ago on a cloak and dagger operation in Eastern Europe and remained close friends ever since.

Coop jumped out of his chair and threw his arms around her. "God, it's good to see you. Where've you been?"

She hugged him back. "Long, boring case in New York. I just got back last week."

He pointed to a chair and patted the seat. "Sit down, sit down. Coffee?"

"Black's good." She took a seat and looked around the room. It didn't accommodate much furniture other than Coop's desk and a few folding chairs. "So, how come the fancy digs?"

"They used to give a gold watch, but now it's a wood-paneled closet."

"Beats my cubicle. So, how're you doing? I looked in on you at the hospital, but you were pretty much out of it. Tubes were sticking out of everywhere."

"Body's fine, but the head's a little screwed up."

"Well, maybe mental health is over-rated. Just ask my grandpa."

Coop laughed. "Hey, catch me up. Are you seeing anyone?"

"No, you know me. A long-term relationship is dinner and a movie. How are you and Fran doing?"

There was no response. Coop just stared off into the distance.

"Oh, Coop, I'm so sorry."

He thought about it for a few seconds. "Don't be. It's my fault. I keep saying I'll fix it, but...hey, I didn't ask you here to unload my baggage."

Zoe set down her cup. "Uh, oh. What's up?" Coop reached for the carafe and started to freshen her coffee. She waved him off. "I'm good."

"I'm going back to Iraq," Coop said.

"Really. Why?"

"Director's got a new bug up his ass over finding Saddam's gold."

"Is your head ready for it?"

"Probably not, but I'll never be right 'til I figure out what happened over there. Got anything on your plate right now?"

"Why? You want me to go with you?"

"If you can swing it."

She gave it a couple seconds before she answered. "Sure, when do we leave?"

"I sense some hesitation," Coop said.

"No, I'm fine with it. I'm just wondering if it's the best thing for you. Maybe you should just move on."

"I appreciate your looking out for me, but I'm going to give it two weeks and then I'll bury it."

A knock on the door interrupted them. Coop didn't make a habit of intimidating people, but when he was annoyed, he didn't hesitate either. "What do ya want? I'm busy," he shouted.

The door was slow to open. A big, somewhat overweight guy in his late thirties stuck his head around it. "Mr. Cooper?"

"Yeah, call me Coop. What d'ya need?"

The guy wasn't sure he was invited into the office, so he stood half in and half out. "I'm Marco Torelli. Deputy Director Nichols sent me over." He waved a manila folder. "Here's my file."

Coop signaled Marco to pull up the remaining chair. "I'm not sure why Randy sent you here," Coop said.

Marco didn't fit very well in the metal chair and rearranged his butt. "Well, he wants...wants me to be part of your team. You know... in Iraq."

Coop took the folder and began skimming through it. Marco turned to Zoe and gave her a sheepish look; she winked back. When Coop was finished, he grabbed his cell phone. "Excuse me, I'll be back in a minute." He stormed out of the office, leaving behind an awkward cloud of silence.

Zoe thrust out her hand. "Zoe Fields, we've never met."

Marco heaved a sigh of relief and reached for her hand. "Marco Torelli. I guess Mr. Cooper isn't too happy with this."

"Oh, don't worry about it, his bark is worse than his bite. I haven't seen you around. Are you new to D.C.?"

"Yes, I'm only a year out of the academy, so I'm new to just about everywhere. I really hope Mr. Cooper will put me on the team. Anything I can do to persuade him?"

"I'd start by dropping the mister. He just goes by Coop."

"Oh, okay, thanks."

Coop tore past the rows of cubicles, ignoring the agents at work and stomped into the hallway. He speed-dialed a number and cocked his anger like a loaded shotgun. When Randy picked up, Coop pulled the trigger. "Randy, what the fuck?"

"What's up?"

"What's up? That Torelli guy. That's what's up."

"So, what's the problem?

"You said I was in charge of this op. I didn't ask for some neophyte to be on board."

"He can learn a lot from you. Cut him some slack."

The decibel level of Coop's voice was rising and an agent opened the office door to see what the commotion was about. Coop gave him the finger and the guy went back inside. "Listen, Randy, I'm not..."

"Director Dutton wants him to go along, so case closed. Hey, good luck over there." Randy hung up.

Coop returned to his office and slammed his phone on the desk. He picked up Marco's file and began reading through it again. Zoe knew Coop well enough to stay quiet while he worked things out and Marco was smart enough to follow her lead and also keep his mouth shut. The process took ten minutes. Coop tossed the folder on the desk and looked at Marco. "Listen buddy, I'll be honest. I'm sure you're a good guy and a good agent, but I don't like having trainees on my missions. Randy knows that, but he doesn't seem to give a shit."

Marco looked like a kid whose ice cream had been snatched away. "I understand, sir. But I promise I'll be a fast learner and if you..."

"Relax, you're on the team. But one fuck-up and you're on the next plane home."

Marco's pout melted away. "Thank you, Mr. Coo...thank you, Coop."

Coop grabbed the Gold Operation folder and a pack of cigarettes from his desk. He offered one to Marco. He held up his hand and took out a package of gum. "No thanks, I quit...gained forty pounds. I use this stuff instead."

"Yeah? Does it work?"

"I'll tell you in six months."

Coop laughed and opened the classified folder. He took out two sets of photos and handed one set to Zoe and the other to Marco. "Okay, here's the deal. Saddam hid a shitload of gold just before he was captured. We're gonna find it."

Zoe looked at the photos. The first one showed a man in his late fifties; his clothes were tailored and expensive. "So, who's the guy in the Armani suit?" she asked.

"That's Cristophe Amacher, a Swiss banker who's done a lot of business in Iraq. He calls it exporting. We call it smuggling. We know he was looking for the gold."

"Maybe he found it," Zoe said.

"Maybe. Maybe not." Coop pointed to the other photo. It showed the face of a tough middle-eastern-looking man glad handing with Saddam Hussein. "This guy is Sahir Ghazali. He was Saddam's number one bodyguard."

"You're thinking he may know where Saddam stashed the gold?" Marco asked.

"He was Saddam's shadow. If anyone would know, he would. The ambassador's office has a file on him."

Zoe handed the photos back to Coop. "We start with him then?"

"Marco and I do. You get Amacher."

Everyone was eager to get started; they agreed to leave the next day. Zoe booked a commercial flight to Zurich, departing at 2:14

p.m. and Coop reserved two seats on a military transport headed to Baghdad at 5:30.

Coop straightened his desk and was getting ready to leave the office when his cell buzzed. He flipped it open. "Coop," he said.

A soft-measured voice responded. "Hello, Mr. Cooper, this is Doctor Goodman. Do you have a minute?"

"Sure Doc, what's up?"

"It's about yesterday's X-rays."

"What? The wound's not healing right?"

"No, the wound is fine. It's the lobe next to it that concerns me."

"Concerns you? What does that mean?"

The doctor cleared his voice. "Well, there's a dark spot on it. I need to do a needle biopsy."

"Can it wait? I'm headed out of the country tomorrow night."

"I'm afraid not, but I can schedule the procedure for eleven tomorrow morning, if that would work for you."

Coop was inclined to bury his head in the sand but thought better of it. "Okay, how will I be afterwards?"

"A little sore, but nothing that will slow you down. How long will you be gone?"

"Hopefully, no more than a week or two."

"Fine. I'll have the results for you as soon as you get back."

"Sounds good, Doc."

"Check in at the Georgetown University Hospital at ten."

Eight

The doc was right. Coop's chest was sore and it hurt when he took a deep breath, but he shook it off and packed a bag. He wanted to write Fran a long letter and try to explain, but he couldn't find the words; instead, he jotted her a short note and left it on the kitchen table. He didn't mention the X-ray results or the biopsy.

The C-17 was the military equivalent of the civilian 747. Two tanks, three jeeps and a helicopter occupied most of the space, but three rows of seats, enough for twelve passengers, were configured near the front of the fuselage. Only Coop, Marco, and one other guy showed up for the flight so they each took a row and sacked out as soon as the pilot leveled off at 28,000 feet.

Coop nudged Marco. "Hey, man. We'll be there in four hours. There's a table of food in the back if you're hungry."

Marco opened his eyes and used the back of his index finger to rub the cobwebs out. He glanced at his watch. He had been asleep for nine hours. "Yeah, that would be great. Let's eat."

If Marco's chewing gum diet was working, his tray didn't show it. He sampled at least one helping of everything. They sat next to each other while they ate. "Is this a dangerous mission?" Marco asked.

Coop took a bite out of an over-steamed fried chicken leg and made a face. "I doubt it. Are you worried?"

"Not really. Randy said you're the best agent he ever worked with."

"Yeah, well, consider the source."

"I'm not sure what you mean."

Coop put his hand on Marco's shoulder. "Look, buddy, a lot of water has flowed under the bridge between Randy and me. I appreciate your trust and you don't have to worry; I'll keep my team safe."

Marco placed his hand over Coop's. "I know you will," he said.

After fourteen hours of sheer boredom, the pilot delivered ten seconds of sheer terror. He double-bounced the 600,000 lb. behemoth onto the runway. Coop and Marco retrieved their duffels from the holding nets and waited impatiently for the door to be opened. When the attendant finally popped it, Baghdad's mid-September air rushed in, filling the compartment with ninety-eight-degree heat. "Feels like a blast furnace," Marco said.

Coop laughed. "Probably a cold front passing through."

The agents descended the portable stairs that had been wheeled to the door of the C-17. Their appearance was the signal for a shiny black SUV, complete with diplomatic plates, to drive across the tarmac and pull to a stop next to the plane. A head poked from the driver's window. "Mr. Cooper?"

He waved his hand and the driver jumped from the car. "Good flight, sir?" he asked.

"Yeah, except for the fried chicken. Where do we throw these duffels?"

"Oh, sorry." The driver grabbed both bags and tossed them into the rear compartment while Coop and Marco settled into the back seats.

Coop gazed out the window. The roads with their bombed pockmarks looked the same, but the soldiers guarding them looked different. When Coop had been there nine months earlier the Americans manned the checkpoints; now it was the Iraqis.

The driver reached the Green Zone and rolled down his window to show credentials. The mixture of smells—stale smoke, garlic and gunpowder—hit Coop like a fist to the gut.

"You okay?" Marco asked.

Coop used the back of his hand to wipe perspiration from his upper lip. "Yeah, sure. Just a little warm, that's all."

The Green Zone was the home for dozens of apartment complexes. Most were occupied by U.S. government workers whose proximity to the embassy was based on the workers' perceived importance. The driver pulled to the front of a building situated right next door to the consulate.

The driver unloaded the duffels and handed Coop a couple of keys. "Third floor, are you guys okay with the bags?"

"Yeah, we're fine. Thanks."

The driver turned to leave and then looked back. "Oh, I almost forgot. Ambassador Billings would like you to drop by as soon as you're settled in."

~ * ~

The news back home was reporting that the war was winding down, but what it didn't say was the violence was not. When they approached the embassy, Coop noticed more soldiers guarding the building today than when he left almost a year ago.

Coop and Marco signed receipts for their weapons and followed a Marine. The ambassador's complex was the garden spot of the Green Zone. It occupied the entire top floor of the embassy building, overlooking the Tigris River to the east and downtown Baghdad to the west.

They stepped into the reception area where the ambassador's secretary had his head buried in a computer. He looked up, did a double take and rushed over to greet Coop with a bear hug. "You're back," he said. "I can't believe it."

"How're you doing, Ted? Staying out of trouble?"

"You mean since the last time?"

Coop laughed. "That was a great night, wasn't it? I'm still hungover."

Ted turned to Marco. "I don't know how he did it, but your buddy here kept me out of a Baghdad jail." He thrust out his hand. "Ted Staley, by the way."

Marco gripped Ted's hand. "Marco Torelli. Coop's showing me the ropes, but I didn't know jail was on the list."

"He's making a lot outa nothing."

"I don't think so," Ted said.

"Hey, we'll catch up later." Coop pointed to the private office. "The big guy's expecting us."

"Okay, great. I'll tell him you're here."

The office had a palatial look, much like it did when it belonged to Saddam. The ambassador hadn't changed much either. He was almost sixty, but a skilled plastic surgeon had been able to knock off ten years, making him look about the same age as Coop. He rose to greet them. "Coop, wonderful to see you again. You look fantastic. How's that hole in your back?"

"Fine, thanks, Mr. Ambassador. I have to say I'm surprised you're still working the Baghdad duty."

"Oh, I love it here. It'll be five years in February."

Coop patted Marco's shoulder. "This is my colleague, Marco Torelli."

Marco shook hands with the ambassador and Billings motioned them to a large conference table where a pecking order was quickly established: Billings at the head, Coop next to him and Marco down line. A steaming pot and a half dozen cups were already on the table. "Tea? I have a wonderful Darjeeling Black Leaf from India," Billings said.

Coop was a coffee guy. He hated tea; even the smell of it turned his stomach. "Sure, that would be great," he said.

Billings filled three cups and passed them down the line. Coop took a sip and swallowed hard. He could never figure out why half the world drank the stuff. He dipped into the sugar and added three teaspoons. Marco must have had the same reaction; he signaled Coop to pass the bowl down.

"How's that for a tea?" Billings said.

"Wonderful." Coop said.

"The best," Marco added.

Billings clasped his hands together on the table and leaned in toward Coop. "So, Randy called and asked me to give you all the help I can."

"Great, we'll need a car and the file you have on a Saddam operative. A guy named Ghazali."

"You know the car's no problem, but that name doesn't ring a bell. Maybe one of my deputies will know who he is."

"Randy said you would have the file. I'd appreciate it if you could get it pulled and ready for me ASAP."

"I'll have it delivered to you in the morning," Billings said. He noticed the cups were empty. "Oh, how rude of me. More tea?"

"No...no thanks, we'll take a raincheck. You know, jet lag and all," Coop said.

Billings stood and extended his hand. "Of course. You men get some rest and I'll talk to you in the morning."

Coop and Marco waited for the elevator to come up from the basement. Marco made an effort at small talk. "Seems like a nice guy."

"You think so?"

"You don't like him?"

"Do you?"

"I don't know him."

The elevator door opened and the two men got in. Coop laughed. "A few words of advice. Be wary of any guy who drinks Darjeeling Black Leaf from India."

Nine

Fatigue was setting in. Coop popped the top off a beer and laid down on the bed, nonchalantly gazing at the chandelier hanging from the twelve-foot ceiling. Five of the candelabra light bulbs were shining bright, but one was flickering. It began to drive him nuts. He chugged the rest of his beer and dragged himself off the bed.

His room had a desk and chair nestled in the corner. Coop pushed the desk alongside the bed and set the chair on top of it. He carefully scaled his makeshift ladder and with an arm stretched to the limit, he was able to reach the flickering bulb. To his surprise, it came out of the socket with a quarter twist. Dropping out behind it came a miniature microphone that hung by a double strand of wire. Coop examined it, then worked it back into the socket and replaced the bulb with a quarter turn.

He grabbed his phone and left his room for the hallway, where he punched in a number and waited. "Ambassador Billing's office. Ted speaking."

"Ted, it's Coop."

"Hey man. What's up?"

"Listen, I need to talk to you."

"Shoot."

"No, not over the phone. Can we meet tonight?"

"Sure. Whereabouts?"

"You remember that place where you got picked up by that good-looking chick?"

For a few seconds, there was no response. "Uh, as I recall, I picked her up."

"That's not how I remember it, but it doesn't matter. How's ten o'clock?"

Coop stepped back into his room and looked up at the chandelier. The light was flickering again. He flipped off the switch, flopped on the bed and passed out for a couple of hours. When he awoke it was a few minutes after nine. He ran through a quick shower and headed out to the restaurant.

He pulled onto a gravel pad that abutted a cinder block building. There was only one other vehicle in the lot—a beat-up van that looked like it had been abandoned during the war. The restaurant was a toss-up between a dump and a dive, but whichever, the dinner rush was over; the place was empty. Coop chose a spot in the back, dropped a folder on the table and sat down to wait for Ted.

Ted arrived five minutes later. He was wearing a pair of old jeans and a T-shirt with the words *I Hate Sand* printed on the front. As usual, he flashed his good-natured smile. "I almost lost you in the crowd."

Coop laughed. "Yeah, I should have worn a flower in my lapel. Hey, where did you get that shirt?"

"Flea market. Ya like it?"

"It's different."

"My favorite," Ted said.

The owner, who doubled as the waiter and probably the cook, lumbered over to the table and pointed toward Coop. "I get you something?"

"A falafel pita and a beer...any beer."

The guy looked at Ted. He held up two fingers. The waiter retreated to the kitchen and Ted leaned in toward Coop. "I'm surprised you came back."

"I have some unfinished business."

"I didn't think you would let it go."

The waiter returned with the beers and the food arrived a couple minutes later. Ted dug into the pita and took a long pull on the beer bottle. "So, other than the fine cuisine, why are we here?"

"I found a bug planted in my ceiling light."

"Yeah, so?"

"You're not surprised?"

"Not really, Billings bugs a lot of the rooms. Especially when the Russians or Chinese are staying there."

"I get that, but why bug me?"

"It's probably a left-over dud."

"I checked. It was hot."

Ted remained unimpressed. "Hey, Billings does a lot of shit I don't understand."

Coop turned over the folder. Even upside-down Ted could decipher the word SECRET. He said, "What a shmuck I am. I actually thought this might be a reunion dinner."

"I love you, man, but I still have a job to do."

"Yeah, I get it. So, what's a classified folder have to do with me?"

Coop opened the folder and laid two photos on the table. "I was hoping you might recognize these guys."

Ted picked up the photos and squinted as he studied the picture of Amacher. "Should I know this guy?"

"Just a shot. I thought maybe he came around the embassy looking for favors or something."

"Sorry, I've never seen him before." Ted handed the photo back to Coop.

"How 'bout the other guy?" Coop asked.

Ted looked at the photo and bit on his lower lip. "I don't know. Maybe."

"Take your time."

Ted took a pair of readers from his pocket and placed them on the bridge of his nose. "I think he may have met with Billings."

"Think?"

"Yeah, I'm pretty sure he did."

"How many times? Once, twice?"

Ted kept staring at the photo. "I don't really remember exactly, but I'm thinking a couple of times. What's his name?"

"Ghazali."

He shook his head. "Huh, that draws a blank."

"Listen, Ted, I need to know why Billings would meet with this guy."

Ted held up his hands. "Uh, uh, this is way above my pay grade."

"Look, I'm not asking you to kill the guy, just nose around Billings' office. You must know where he stashes his private stuff."

"Yeah, maybe, but I'm not a spy. I could get hung out to dry or worse yet...hung."

Coop laughed. "Spying? This isn't spying. It's like sneaking a chocolate chip from a cookie."

"No, I can't..."

"You said you owe me, remember—for keeping you out of jail."

"Yeah, but I was thinking about buying you a beer, not risking my ass."

"I'll make it up to you."

"How?"

"I don't know. Maybe I'll buy you a decent T-shirt."

Ted pushed away from the table. "I'll think about it. I have to hit the head."

Coop placed the photos back in the folder and dropped two twenties on the table. When Ted returned, Coop waved the file. "Well?"

Ted frowned. "It still doesn't feel right. Give me some more time to think about it?"

"I was hoping you could check it out tonight."

Ted's eyes opened wide and his eyebrows lifted up. "You're kidding? Tonight?"

"Look, I don't have a lot of time. Randy only funded this operation for a couple weeks."

Ted wiped a couple dots of perspiration from his forehead. "If I do it...goddammit...you can't ask me again."

"I promise," Coop said.

They walked to the parking lot. A bright yellow Toyota was parked between Coop and the old van. "Is that yours?" Coop asked, pointing to the lemon-colored car.

"Yeah, you like it?"

"Love it." Coop handed Ted his business card. It identified him as an American business consultant from Des Moines, Iowa. "Call me if you find anything."

Ted agreed and drove away. Coop fired up his engine and looked over his shoulder to back out around the van. He slammed on the brake. He thought he saw movement inside the clunker. He put his car in PARK, approached the van's passenger window and cupped his hands over his temples to look inside. A mound of electronic wires and several miniature microphones were piled on the seat, but he couldn't see all the way to the back and couldn't make out if anyone was inside. He returned to his car and drove off.

Ten

It was after midnight by the time Ted entered the lobby of the embassy. The night guard was doing his best to stay awake and was on the tail end of a yawn when Ted approached his desk. The guard looked up. "Working late?" he asked.

Even though the guard recognized him, Ted knew he would have to show his credentials. He dropped them on the desk. "Yeah, the ambassador needs some stuff done by morning."

The guard logged Ted in and handed back his documents. "Pretty lonely tonight."

"No one else around?"

"Nope. Just you."

Ted thanked him and took the elevator to the top floor. The guard was right. All the offices were dark, the hall was empty and the lights were dimmed to their lowest level. He rummaged through a ring of keys until he found the one to the ambassador's front-office door. He entered the dark reception area and headed straight to Billings' private office. He sorted through the keys again, unlocked the door and stepped into a place where he knew he shouldn't be.

One wall was floor to ceiling cabinets that were veneered to blend in with the décor. Ted began with the top cabinet and worked his way down. He sorted through old computer printouts, outdated files and years of old appointment books. An hour and a half of searching brought no results.

He turned his attention to Billings' mahogany desk. Everything on the polished top was arranged in the perfect order one would expect from a neat-freak. He knew Billings and knew none of those items bore any importance. He began sorting through the drawers. The top one was filled with supplies: pens, pencils, clips and other assorted junk. The middle drawer held personal items: a couple bottles of cologne, a six-pack of condoms and an 8 x 10 photograph. Ted turned the photo over. There was an inscription on the back. He set it on the desk.

The bottom drawer was locked. Ted sorted through his keys, but none was small enough to fit the lock. He spotted a metal letter opener, picked it up and began wedging it between the drawer and the casing. Ted froze; the silence in the empty building was suddenly broken by the sound of a door closing. It echoed from the hallway.

Ted turned off the room light and waited in the dark with the letter opener in hand, not knowing what he'd do with it if someone entered. He remained still for five minutes. The room was quiet, and no more sounds were coming from the hall. He thought maybe he imagined it; maybe this spy stuff was getting to him.

He went back to work. He wiggled the opener blade between the drawer and the casing until it struck metal, then pushed as hard as he could. The drawer popped open. He sorted through a pile of letters and documents. Nothing appeared important enough to be under lock and key until he spotted a manila folder labeled: FRIENDS.

The folder was filled with photos; he began sorting through them. One face looked familiar. He turned the photo over. There was writing on the back. He smiled and set the photo on the desk next to the one he had found in the other drawer. He took out his phone along with Coop's business card.

Coop's phone buzzed. He checked the ID. "Ted?"

"Yeah, Coop, I'm in Billings' office. I found a couple photos you'll be interested in."

"Meet me at that all-night coffee house near the river? Twenty minutes," Coop said.

Ted looked at his watch; if he hurried, he could wind this up in five minutes. He set the photos side by side and engaged the camera on his phone, but before he could snap the pictures, he heard another noise, much louder and much closer than the last. It appeared to come from the hallway right outside of Billings' front office. Adrenalin hit Ted like it had been mainlined into his bloodstream. He broke out in a sweat and his hands began to shake uncontrollably. Try as he may, he couldn't hold his phone steady. He did his best to snap pictures of both sides of the photos and, still shaking badly, he placed them back in the drawers.

~ * ~

The coffee house looked the same as it had when Coop had been there a year ago. Even the five guys embalming themselves with thick brown liquid looked the same. Coop took a table in the corner and lit up a cigarette. He checked the time. It was 2:21 a.m.

After four cups of coffee, Coop's bladder was ready to burst. He looked around the room; everyone was long gone except for the young kid dozing behind the counter. He fumbled through his pack for a cigarette, but they were gone, too. Coop took another look at his watch: 3:38 a.m. He stood up and left.

Eleven

Zurich's main street, the Bahnhofstrasse, was covered with snow from an early winter storm that hit the day before Zoe arrived. It was still snowing lightly the next day when she emerged from a taxi and glanced up the street that was lined with some of the world's most expensive and exclusive shops. She wore makeup, leather gloves, high boots, and a fur coat; her right hand held a leather briefcase. An attendant saw her approaching and swung open the door of the 19th century Swiss Commerce Bank building.

The executive offices occupied the top floor. Zoe stepped from the elevator and entered a door marked: *Lara Graf, Vice President*. A professionally dressed receptionist escorted her to an inner office.

An attractive blonde woman in her early fifties, wearing tailored clothes and expensive jewelry, stepped from behind her desk and extended her hand. "Ms. Rawlings, I am Lara Graf. Please, have a seat."

Zoe removed her fur. A red cashmere sheath hugged every curve of her trim figure. She sat facing Lara. "I'm impressed. I didn't expect a vice president," she said.

"I am in charge of our North American Division. If a client comes to us from the United States, they will pass through my office. May I offer you tea or coffee?"

"Tea is fine. Thank you."

The receptionist, who was keeping a polite distance, poured two cups and left the room. Lara waited until the door completely closed. "I understand you're from Charleston."

"Yes, have you been there?"

"Actually, I have. I received my Masters at Harvard. A few friends and I went down there for a weekend. Quite lovely."

"Yes, it is. If you ever return, you must let me give you a tour."

"That would be wonderful." Lara clasped her hands together. "So, Ms. Rawlings, what can we do to earn our fee today?"

"You can start by calling me Kate."

"Certainly, Kate. And please...I'm Lara."

Zoe opened her briefcase and took out a business-size folder. She slid it across the desk. "My parents died two years ago and left me an inheritance. The taxes on the income are staggering."

Lara slipped on a pair of half-framed readers and leafed through the contents of the folder. She looked over the top of the glasses. "I am so sorry about your parents. I assume you are looking for tax shelter here in Switzerland."

"I heard Swiss Commerce specializes in that."

"Yes, we are very good in this area. It looks as though you have an annual income of over a million dollars, but taxes eat up almost half of it."

"That's about right."

"Kate, this is a common problem. Are you able to stay for a couple days while I devise a strategy for you?"

"I can stay as long as it takes."

"Wonderful." Lara peeked at the old grandfather clock in the corner. "You must be hungry. Have you ever had Swiss veal and potato *rosti*?"

Zoe cocked her head and thought for a few seconds. "I can't say that I have."

"Then you will be my guest. I think you will find it extraordinary." Lara pushed the intercom button. "Greta, our coats please."

Lara and Zoe stepped into the elevator. As the door began to close, a well-manicured hand reached in from the outside and the doors re-opened. A suave, gray-haired man squeezed in next to them. "Oh, Lara, what a surprise. A guest, I assume?"

"Forgive me," Lara said. "This is my new client from America, Kate Rawlings. Kate, this is Christophe Amacher."

He smiled, revealing a sizeable investment in porcelain caps. Zoe extended her hand to shake with Amacher, but instead, he took it in both hands and kissed the top of it. "My pleasure, Ms. Rawlings. Mmm...Chanel Number Five?"

"Nineteen," Zoe said.

"Exquisite."

She withdrew her hand. "Thank you, Mr. Amacher."

"I trust Lara is taking good care of you."

"Excellent care."

"Wonderful, wonderful."

The elevator doors opened into the lobby. Amacher looked at his watch. "Oh, oh, I'm afraid I'm late. It was a pleasure to meet you, Ms. Rawlings. If I can be of any service, don't hesitate to drop by my office." He waved and hurried off.

Zoe laughed and looked at Lara. "Your boss?"

"No, God, no. He is in charge of our Middle East division. We work together on a project now and then."

"That must be loads of fun."

"I apologize for him. He can be a bit patronizing."

Zoe rolled her eyes. "A bit?"

Now it was Lara's turn to laugh. "He has that effect on women. Does he not?"

A sizeable number of heads, mainly men's, turned as the two women—Lara in lynx, Zoe in mink—strolled along the boulevard to the restaurant.

The lobby was packed with patrons who were lining up for tables with the hope of getting lucky. The *maître d'* spotted Lara coming through the door. He worked his way through the crowd and kissed the top of her hand. "*Gueten Abend, Frau* Graf." Lara whispered something in his ear and slipped a large bill into his hand. The *maître d'* discreetly dropped it into his pocket and led them to a quiet table in the back of the dining room.

Lara did the ordering, including several bottles of wine. By the time the appetizers were gone, the Chardonnay was also; the small talk waned. "You're not married?" Lara asked.

Zoe didn't answer and the conversation came to a standstill.

Lara touched the top of Zoe's hand. "Oh, I'm so sorry, that was a very inappropriate question. Quite presumptuous on my part." she said.

"No. No, it's fine," Zoe said. "My mind was just drifting. No, I'm not married. All the men I meet have agendas that I'm not interested in being a part of."

The head waiter arrived and opened a bottle of Burgundy to pair with the veal that was being placed on the table. He waited for Lara to approve the first pour and then filled Zoe's glass. "*Bon appetit*," he said.

When the waiters were out of earshot Zoe said, "I notice you're not wearing a ring either."

Lara cut into the tender meat and mixed a piece with the crisp *rosti* potatoes. "I tried it once...another banker. I knew he wasn't as smart as me, but he thought he was a genius. I went along with the charade until I couldn't handle his stupidity any longer. We were divorced on our one-year anniversary. That was the best day of my life."

Zoe laughed and drained another glass of red the waiter had discreetly poured. By the time the dessert wine arrived, both women were talking loudly and giggling hysterically. The waiter hovered nearby. "I think he wants to go home," Zoe said.

Lara looked at her watch. Her eyes were heavy from the alcohol, but the numbers on the watch were large enough to decipher 11:25 p.m. "Oh my, this evening has passed quickly. I have enjoyed it very much."

"I have too. You were right," Zoe said. "The food was fantastic."

"I come here when I want to impress."

"And you wanted to impress me?"

"Yes, I did."

"And why was that?"

Through lazy eyes, Lara looked at Zoe. "I think you know why." She signaled for their coats and signed the check. "We will share a taxi and I can drop you at your hotel," she said.

The Hotel Baur au Lac catered to wealth and in Zurich, there was plenty of it. Zoe had one of the old-style rooms with a four-poster bed and overstuffed furniture. The sun was coming up and beginning to spray light into the room. Lara, dressed in a bathrobe, held a cup of coffee in both hands as she took in the view of Lake Zurich and the Alps off in the distance. She raised her voice a little. "This hotel is charming. Most Americans seem to gravitate to the Hilton or the Marriott."

Zoe was in the bathroom. "Oh, you're awake. I'll be right out."

"Take your time," Lara said.

Zoe stepped into the bedroom. She too was dressed in a hotel robe. She settled in behind Lara and put her arms around her waist. "Well, that was an unexpected evening."

"It was, wasn't it. Tell me, Kate, do you do this often?"

"What do you mean?"

"Have one-night stands."

"What makes you think this is a one-night stand?" Zoe asked.

Lara turned and faced Zoe. "I'm a realist. In a week, you will be back in the States and I will be here in Zurich."

"It's only an eight-hour flight. I'll be back. I promise."

Twelve

Coop wasn't crazy about the food in the embassy cafeteria, but since he rarely had anything more than coffee for breakfast, and since Marco tended to choose quantity over quality, this place would do. Coop was on his second cup.

Marco spotted Coop in the corner and hustled over. He set his tray on the table. It was loaded with eggs, bacon, sausage, cheese, and buttered toast. "Did they have any Lipitor to go with that?" Coop said.

Marco wrinkled his forehead. "I don't get it."

"Never mind—bad joke."

"Did Billings send that file over?" Marco asked.

"Not yet. I was hoping he'd at least have called by now." Coop punched a few numbers into his cell and waited for an answer. A man's voice answered. "Ted?" Coop said.

"I'm sorry, Ted isn't here today."

"Oh, is he sick?"

"I don't know, sir. May I leave him a message?"

"Actually, I'm calling for Ambassador Billings. Could you tell him Craig Cooper's on the line?"

The receptionist put Coop on hold, where he was left to listen to elevator music. He was well aware of Billings' many affectations and overworking the hold button was one of his favorites. Coop checked his watch; he'd been holding for five minutes. A few seconds later Billings came on the line. "Coop, what can I do for you?"

"Mr. Ambassador, good morning. I was hoping you could shoot me that file I asked for. We'd like to get going on it."

"Oh, that. No one's been able to locate it."

"That's strange, Randy checked with your office a few days ago and they said you had it."

"Well, we can't seem to find it and no one has time right now to..."

Coop rolled his eyes. "Excuse me. Could someone find the time?" Billings didn't answer. Coop said it again, "Mr. Ambassador, could someone find the time...please?"

"We're a little short-staffed so..."

"So what? You promised me that file."

Confrontations were not Billings' strong suit; Coop waited him out. After what seemed like an eternity, Billings spoke. "As a special favor, I'll get someone on it."

"Thank you, sir." Coop slammed the phone on the table. "Pompous prick."

Marco's mouth was full of food. "We 'ave a probum?"

Coop pulled the tray away from him. "Get over there and make a pest of yourself till someone comes up with that file. I'll meet you at the motor pool." Marco plucked one last sausage from his plate and hustled toward the door.

Coop finished his coffee and took the elevator down to the motor pool. When the doors opened, he gazed into the garage; his hands began to tremble and his stomach cramped. The last time he left the Green Zone from this motor pool, he returned inside an ambulance with an EMT putting pressure on the wound in his back. He still wasn't clear on the details, but he did remember being operated on and airlifted to Germany before being sent back to D.C.

Billings kept his word on at least one promise; the motor pool had a car reserved for Coop. He took a seat on the passenger side while waiting for Marco and lit a cigarette, but after one puff, he threw it out the window.

The elevator doors opened and Marco, chewing a wad of gum, entered the motor pool garage. He looked around and spotted a cubicle where the attendant was slumped over with his head buried in a cell phone. Marco approached and tapped on the glass. "Hey, you awake in there?"

The attendant snapped the phone shut and came to attention. "Sorry, sir...Oh, hi. I haven't seen you in a while. How have you been?"

"I've been fine." Marco performed a quick survey of the garage. "I'm looking for my partner. A good-looking guy...probably puffing on a cigarette."

"Oh, you must mean agent Cooper." The attendant pointed to a row of cars. "He's over there in the gray Ford."

Marco thanked him and strolled to the car where Coop was leaning back in the passenger seat with his eyes closed. The discarded cigarette, still burning, was on the cement next to the car door. Marco settled into the driver's seat and slammed the door. Coop's eyes popped open. "Oh, you're here."

"Yeah, what's with the unsmoked cigarette?"

"I just quit. Did you get the file?"

Marco reached into his pants pocket, pulled out a single piece of notepaper and handed it to Coop. He turned it over a couple times. "An address? That's it?"

Marco shrugged.

"What an asshole," Coop muttered. "Okay, you drive. It's in Karbala."

Marco pulled out of the garage and headed south. When he saw a sign for Route 8, he took a left and joined the highway. "You know the way?" Coop asked.

"I kinda checked it out on my way down the elevator."

Traffic moved along nicely at 88 kph for the first thirty-five kilometers but slowed to a crawl as half a dozen soldiers directed traffic past an overturned Humvee smoldering by the side of the road. Coop caught Marco staring at two body bags lying next to it. "Hey, buddy, keep your eyes on the road. Trust me, you'll see worse before we leave this hell hole."

Karbala wasn't hard to find, it was only ninety-eight kilometers southwest of Baghdad, but finding Ghazali's house, that was a problem. Over a million people lived in the area and it was obvious that no city planner had been hired to lay it out. Some streets were so narrow, two-way traffic was impossible; others led to an abrupt dead-end. Most were poorly marked in Arabic or had no signage at all.

Coop opened the glove compartment, pulled out a street map and did his best to match up the address to something on the map. "It's on the other side of town," he said. "It may take a while."

He gave Marco directions, but he picked the wrong street and they found themselves trapped behind a pushcart that had no intention of moving over for an American car. They crawled along for twenty minutes until Marco seized an opportunity and gunned the Ford past the vendor. They sped off and made good time until traffic brought them to a halt once again. Slowly, they crisscrossed the city until they reached a gravel road on the east side. Coop pointed to a small house up ahead. "That must be it." Marco came to a stop in front of a cinder-block structure with a shingle-covered pitched roof.

A dog barked and ran circles around them as they approached the front door, but he lost interest after Coop patted him on the head and told him what a good boy he was. Coop rapped on the door and noticed the curtains over the front window part just a hair. He knocked again and this time the door opened a crack and an old woman peeked out and began rattling off words in Arabic.

"Sahir Ghazali?" Coop said. The woman stopped speaking and gave him a blank stare. Coop dug into his meager cache of language skills. "*Titkallam Ingliza?*

The woman shook her head. "No. No *Ingliza*."

He printed the name Sahir Ghazali on the back of the address note and held it up in front of the woman. She shook her head again.

"*Shukran*," Coop said and returned with Marco to the car.

When they were settled back in the front seats, Coop lit up a cigarette. "Thought you quit," Marco said.

"That was two hours ago. Did Billings give you this address or did Ted?"

"Ted wasn't there. It was Billings."

Coop threw his cigarette out the window and turned to Marco. "Got a piece of that gum?"

Marco unwrapped a stick of Juicy Fruit and handed it to Coop, who shoved it into his mouth and leaned back with his eyes closed. The inside of the car was getting hot; Marco started the engine and cranked up the AC. The noise reenergized the dog and he jumped against the car door and began barking again. Marco unwrapped another stick of gum and threw it out the window. The dog picked it up with his tongue and spit it out. Marco laughed. "Stupid mutt."

The barking woke Coop from his self-induced trance. "Did you see any police stations in this town?" he asked.

Marco thought for a minute. "Yeah, I think so. A couple of miles back, maybe."

It's always a lot easier getting into a maze than it is getting out. After a dozen turns, they found themselves on a narrow street behind another line of pushcarts. Marco honked the horn, but nobody so much as turned around. After creeping along behind the vendors for a mile or two, Coop pointed to a building with a red, white and green flag out front. "There, pull up over there." He got out of the car and went inside the building.

A half-dozen police officers were huddled around an old iMac, laughing and pointing at the computer screen. The man operating the keyboard spotted Coop, said something to the others and turned off the computer. The room went silent and the officers dispersed. Coop approached the man seated behind the computer and took out his identification along with his gold shield. "English?" he asked.

The officer tweaked his mustache. "I may help you?"

Coop unfolded the paper with the name Sahir Ghazali written on it and handed it to the officer. "I'm looking for the address of this man. He lives here in Karbala. Any chance you might have him in your database?"

The policeman turned his computer back on. The photo of a naked girl appeared on the screen and he quickly changed windows. "It is possible," he said. He hunted and pecked his way around the keys until a new window lit up the screen. It showed rows and rows of names, dates, and addresses. He scrolled a couple pages. "Your friend is a busy man, Mr. Cooper."

"How so?"

"He spends much time in our police stations." The officer scribbled an address on the back of an envelope and handed it to Coop. "To drive in Karbala is very difficult. I will give you directions," he said.

Coop thanked the man and headed back to the car. Marco somehow managed to find an American country music station and was tapping his fingers on the dash, keeping time with Carrie Underwood. Coop opened the passenger door. "Let's go."

Marco turned off the radio and started the engine. "You got something?"

"Yeah, take a left at the corner."

The house, more like a shack, was located on the outskirts of Karbala. It was one of about a dozen structures that were squeezed together on a piece of sandy real estate. Marco turned off the engine and scanned the area. "I'll tell you one thing. If he knows where the gold is stashed, he hasn't dug into it."

"Yeah, not exactly Park Avenue, is it?" Coop said.

Their shoes kicked up dust as they approached the house. Coop knocked on the door, but there was no response. He made a fist and banged the heel of his hand on the door. "Hello? Anybody here?"

"Doesn't look like it," Marco said.

Coop made his way to the side of the house and motioned to Marco. "Check the back."

The constant blowing of dust caused several layers of grime to build on the windows. Coop spit on his hand and used it to buff out a spot. He looked inside. A small TV with a rabbit-ears antenna was flickering, but no one was watching it. He moved along to the next window. Before he could spit-clean this one, Marco shouted from the rear of the house.

"Coop...Coop, come back here." He hustled to where Marco had his hands cupped next to his temples and was looking through a window. "Check this out," Marco said.

He took Marco's spot and peered through the window. It was hard to see inside, but he was able to make out the back of a man sitting at a kitchen table. He rapped on the window. The man didn't turn around. Coop made a beeline for the front door with Marco trailing close behind. Coop took out his pistol and used the metal butt to bang on the door. "Ghazali...U.S. agents...open the door," he shouted.

To Coop's surprise, the door was unlocked. He opened it and stormed into the hallway. Marco drew his pistol and followed. Coop shouted in the direction of the kitchen, "Ghazali? Sahir Ghazali?" No one answered.

Coop motioned toward the kitchen and started down the hall. Marco scanned the surroundings and leveled his pistol to cover Coop as they moved forward. Coop raised his Glock to eye level, grasped it with both hands and burst into the kitchen. "U.S. agents," he hollered.

The man hadn't moved; he was still sitting at the table. It was Ghazali. His eyes were open and he had a bullet hole in his forehead.

Thirteen

Red and blue strobes flashed from the tops of police cars lined up along the riverbank. A tow truck, with a chain attached to its rear bumper, backed up to the edge of the water. A diver popped his head above the surface and waved. The truck driver waved back. He forced the transmission into low gear and the truck strained to gain traction. As the tires dug in, it moved forward and a car slowly emerged from beneath the surface of the water. Even with mud dripping from it, the color was obvious. It was bright yellow.

Coop was in REM sleep when his cellphone buzzed. He fumbled around and managed to grab it before it vibrated onto the floor. He checked the time. It was 1:35 a.m.

"Cooper," he answered. "When?" he asked. "Oh shit," he said. "I'll be there in ten minutes."

The morgue inside the Green Zone initially took up one floor of an old medical clinic. With all the deaths from road bombs and the deadly attacks against the military, it had been expanded to occupy all three stories. The attendant, the same one who called Coop, escorted him to a room that was decorated in contemporary wall-to-wall stainless steel. He pulled out a drawer and slid the sheet off the body. The dead man was wearing a T-shirt— *I Hate Sand.*

Coop tried to swallow, but the lump in his throat felt like a baseball. He bit his lower lip. "How did you happen to call me?"

"He had your card in his pocket. Is there anyone else we should notify?"

"Yeah, he worked for Ambassador Billings."

"Thanks, we'll call him in the morning."

"How did it happen?" Coop asked.

"A car accident. He must have gone off the road and into the river."

"When?"

"We're not really sure. The water level dropped this evening and someone spotted the back of the car."

"Damn. He was a good guy."

The attendant's voice took on the tone of an undertaker selling a casket. "Take as much time...as much...you know, as you need." He let the door close quietly behind him, leaving Coop alone with Ted.

He slipped his hands into Ted's jean pockets. They were empty. He looked around the room and spotted a pile of plastic bags stacked on a nearby counter. He sorted through them until he found the one marked 'Theodore Staley.' He turned it upside down. A phone, a wallet, and a ring of keys fell onto the counter.

Coop looked through the wallet. There wasn't much: a California driver's license, a couple of credit cards, some wet Iraqi currency, and a few soaked U.S. bills. He picked up the cell phone and hit the power button. It was as dead as Ted.

The only thing left were the keys. Coop turned them over in his hand and dropped them into his pocket along with the phone. He re-covered Ted with the sheet. "God, I'm sorry buddy...really sorry."

Fourteen

Coop rinsed his razor in the sink and inspected his face in the mirror. He wasn't sure, but it looked like a couple new wrinkles were forming on his forehead. Someone knocked on the apartment door. "It's open," Coop said.

Marco came in, popped his gum twice and sat down. "You wanted to talk to me?"

"Yeah, I have some personal stuff to take care of, so you're on your own today."

"You need a driver or something?"

"No, I'm good," Coop said. Marco's expression took on a hangdog look. "Hey," Coop said. "Why don't you sign for a car and check out downtown? Maybe meet some locals. They're really good people."

Marco mulled it over for a few minutes. "Okay, I might do that."

Coop took the elevator to the basement of the embassy building where the Records Room, that was appropriately nicknamed the Dungeon, was located. As he walked from the elevator, the custodian, a matronly woman whose glasses dangled from a chain and rested on her mammoth breasts, looked up from her computer. "May I help you?" she said, watching Coop approach.

He showed her his photo ID. "Yeah, I need access to a computer."

The woman put on her glasses and inspected the plastic card. "I haven't seen you here before. Are you new?"

"Not exactly, I was stationed here for a while, but I left about a year ago."

"Well, welcome back to Paradise." Coop hoped she was kidding. She handed him a sheet of instructions and said, "This will walk you through. The password's good for twenty-four hours."

He took the first seat in a row of computers. He entered his password and typed in 12/30/2006. The screen lit up—ACCESS DENIED. He slid over to the next computer and followed the same procedure, but it yielded the same result. He returned to the custodian's desk. "This password doesn't work. I can't get into one of the databases."

The woman adjusted her glasses and opened a window on her screen. "What date was that?"

"December thirtieth, 2006."

She tapped a few keys and studied the screen. "Oh, I'm sorry, Mr. Cooper, the ambassador's office has restricted access to that date. Can I help you with another date?"

"No, I need that one."

"I'm sorry, there's nothing I can do. You'll need special authorization."

"Special authorization? I have special...never mind."

Coop stormed out. He started for the elevator, but changed his mind and took the stairs two at a time until he reached the top floor. Out of breath, he rushed past an unfamiliar assistant who was sitting at Ted's desk and burst into Billings' office.

Billings looked up from his desk. "Cooper? What the hell are you doing, barging in like this?"

"You've locked me out."

"Locked you out? Locked you out of where?"

Coop used his shirt sleeve to wipe the sweat from his forehead. "You know damn well where...the database for December thirtieth. I need to see that report."

"Calm down. I don't have anything to do with those databases. Randy must have been the one who set up the restriction."

"Well, you're the ambassador. Remove it."

"I can't. Besides, I don't see how that report is even important to your assignment."

"Really." Coop narrowed his eyes and stared at Billings. "Well, it is, and I'll decide what's important to my assignment. Not you."

"I'm sorry, I'd like to help, but I don't have anything to do with Agency protocols."

A Marine summoned by the startled assistant entered Billings' office. "Any problem, sir?"

"No, no problem. Agent Cooper was just leaving."

Coop turned his back on the ambassador and stomped out. The hallway was empty. He speed-dialed his cell and waited. A sleepy voice answered. "Who...who's calling?"

"Goddammit, Randy, it's Coop."

"Coop? It's three o'clock in the morning here."

"I don't give a shit. Why'd you lock me out of the December thirtieth database?"

"I have no idea what you're talking about. I didn't lock you out of anything."

"Well, Billings said you did."

"I don't know why, but he's lying."

"Look, if you want to get into a pissing contest with Billings, that's your business, but I want access to that database. And damnit, I want it right now."

"I'll take care of it."

"You better." Coop snapped his phone shut.

He needed to calm down and got out of the elevator at the cafeteria level. He ordered a cup of decaf and a doughnut with some sort of jelly oozing out and waited for the pulse beating through his temples to return to normal. He decided to take the stairs to the basement.

The defender of the Dungeon saw him coming and put her glasses back on. "Oh, Mr. Cooper, the ambassador called. He said he was sorry about the mix-up. You're good to go."

Coop thanked her and sat at the same computer he'd used a half-hour earlier. He typed in 12/30/2006. This time the window opened up.

Incident Report Summary:
Randy Nichols, Station Chief
Dec. 30, 2006: 11:48 p.m.
Baghdad: Sadr City District
Informant, Omar Mustafa: shot and killed
Agent, Craig Cooper: shot, critical condition.
Shooter: Unknown
Conclusion: Terrorist attack

Coop banged the table. "Terrorist, my ass."

A voice said, "Are you all right, sir?" Coop looked up. The custodian was standing over him.

"Yeah, just fine," he said. "I'll be done in a minute." He scrolled the screen, found the address he was looking for and jotted it on a piece of paper.

Coop signed out the same gray Ford he and Marco had taken to Karbala the day before and merged with the traffic heading downtown. He eyed the rear-view mirror and noticed a black Honda following three car lengths behind. It hadn't changed its position since Coop entered the boulevard a couple of miles back.

His phone buzzed. He checked the ID and opened it. "Fran? Is everything okay?"

"We haven't heard from you."

"Sorry, it's been hectic."

"Too hectic to call?"

"I'm really sorry. I apologize."

"I can handle it, but Josh has been waiting."

"Damn. Put him on the phone."

"He went to the Wizards' game with a bunch of friends and their dads." Coop felt a sinking feeling work through his body. "Are you there?" Fran said.

"Yeah, yeah I'm here. The cell must have hit a dead spot. I'll call tomorrow. Is this a good time?"

"Fine. I'll make sure he's here...Coop, he misses you a lot."

"I miss him, too. I miss you both."

There was an awkward silence. Fran broke it. "I threw out your boards and all your notes."

"That's fine. Listen, Fran, I know this isn't the best time, but I want to expl..."

Fran cut him off. "You said it's a short assignment. It's been more than a week."

"Yeah, I know, but a lot of shit is hitting the fan over here. It may take a little long..."

Fran interrupted again. "I have to go. The soup's boiling over."

"Oh, okay. I'll talk to you tomorrow then." Fran hung up without saying goodbye. Coop stared at the phone before setting it on the console.

Traffic on Al Rasheed Street, Baghdad's main drag, was heavy. Coop spotted a parking spot in front of the Smoke Shop and snatched it. He looked in his mirror just in time to see the black Honda grab a spot five spaces back.

The shop hadn't changed much since Coop had been there last. Even the layer of smoke that clung to the ceiling looked the same except around the light fixture, where an extra coating of tar blurred the light.

Sami, the owner, was leaning on the counter reading a newspaper as he always did. His salt and pepper hair was uncombed, and it was apparent his razor hadn't been used for days. When Coop entered, Sami looked up from the daily news. "Mr. Coop, I haven't seen you for maybe a year. I think maybe you quit the habit."

"I wish. I've been in the States. How are you doin', Sami? Still working the system?"

Sami grinned, revealing a shiny gold tooth in the front of his mouth. "You mix me up with someone else. Me, I only sell cigars and cigarettes." He reached into a cabinet for an old cigar box and took out a dark brown stogie. "On the house. You like it, I'll make you a good deal."

"Thanks," Coop said. He looked around the room. A big guy, sporting a nose that took one punch too many, was in the corner smoking a cigar as he sized Coop up. The air was getting thicker every time he exhaled. "I'll smoke it out front. 'Let you know how it tastes." Coop stepped outside.

The cigar discharged a dark cloud when Coop lit up. He knew he should snuff it, but he took a chance and inhaled. The thick smoke burned its way down his trachea and set off a coughing fit. When the paroxysm subsided, he peered up the street. The black Honda was still parked, but he could only make out the silhouette of the driver. He put the cigar out under his shoe and walked back inside. "Not bad," he said. "How much for the box?"

Sami slid the carton across the counter. "For you? Twenty dollars."

Coop handed him a hundred-dollar bill. "I'll also need a car for a couple hours."

Sami signaled the big guy, who rose and lumbered his way to the counter. Sami handed him a set of keys. "Take Mr. Coop out back and make him comfortable in my car."

Coop followed the bodyguard to the alley where a fifteen-year-old Corolla was parked. He tossed the cigar box into a trash can and slid onto the driver's seat. After two minutes of cranking the starter, the engine sputtered and began to idle. The engine oil light vacillated between green and red, but finally decided on green. Coop put the clunker in gear and headed to the address he had found earlier on the computer report.

It took Coop about forty-five minutes to get from downtown to a neighborhood of apartment buildings, most of which were covered with Arabic graffiti. But one, the one he was looking for, was somehow spared from the artist's spray can. He parked and went inside.

An old man responded to Coop's knock, but opened the door barely wide enough for a conversation.

"English," Coop asked.

"Little...maybe," the old man answered.

"I'm looking for Ahmad Bishara."

"He move. Almost a year ago."

"Do you know where he went?"

"No," the old man said. He started to close the door.

Coop wedged his shoe between the door and the jamb. "Please, I'm a friend."

The old man looked frightened. "He doesn't want..."

Coop eased the door back open. He took out his wallet and held up a photo of himself with Ahmad. They were smiling and their arms were locked over each other's shoulders. He handed his cell phone to the man. "Tell him Coop is here."

The address the old man gave Coop led him to a slightly better neighborhood; at least it had no graffiti. He knocked and a pretty woman wearing a scarf over her head opened the door. "You are Coop?"

"Yes, I am."

"Please, please come in."

Second-hand furniture was spread neatly through the one-bedroom apartment. Coop peeked into the living room; Ahmad was there, smiling ear to ear. They just stared at each other for a moment before extending their arms for an embrace.

Ahmad took a step back to look at Coop. "You made it," he said.

"Because of you, I heard."

"I wasn't sure I'd ever see you again. You looked pretty bad when I dropped you off in the emergency room."

"I'm fine now. How're you? Still an interpreter?"

"Not since that night."

Ahmad's wife brought in a pot of coffee and a plate of plain white cookies. She poured two cups, set down the sweets and left the room.

Coop sampled the thick brown mixture. "So, why did you quit your job?"

"The informant was assassinated, you were shot, and the next day a man came looking for me. Luckily my wife and I weren't home."

"A man. What man?"

"A *Mujrm*. You know, like a mobster. We moved that evening."

"I'm sorry. Is there any work at all for you?"

"Not really. I doubt the embassy would take me back after I quit so abruptly."

"It's worth a try."

Ahmad frowned. "I'll be all right...I guess."

"Hey, buddy, I need to know what happened that night. How well do you remember it?"

"Like yesterday." He closed his eyes. "I saw a flash from the second floor of the building next to us and before I could even blink, the poor bastard took a bullet in his neck. He was dead before he hit the ground."

"The last thing I remember was Randy telling us to hug the dirt," Coop said.

"Yes, we did that and then scrambled toward the car and then... then you got hit." Ahmad closed his eyes again. "But the shot that hit you...it sounded different."

"Different? What d'ya mean different?"

"I can't say exactly, but it just didn't sound the same."

"Same as what?"

"It didn't sound like the shot that hit the informant...and then a third shot, like the one that got you, hit the car right over my head."

Coop's eyes widened. "What? A third shot? Meant for you?"

Ahmad rubbed his chin. "Who knows, but that's why we moved when that thug showed up at our door."

Coop didn't press further. "Okay, I get it." He took a sip of coffee. "Ahmad, help me out here. Why did you guys leave me lying in the dirt?"

"Randy said you were dead and ordered me to get us the hell out of there. But I saw you go down and I didn't think you were dead, so I went back later to see for myself."

"I never got a chance to thank you."

"It's not necessary. If the circumstances were reversed, you would have come back for me."

"Just the same...thanks." Coop finished his coffee and stood to leave. "Listen Ahmad, the gold operation's been re-opened. I'm going to Tikrit and I'll need an interpreter."

Fifteen

Coop headed back to the Smoke Shop and made a pass in front of it. His car was still where he left it, but the Honda was gone. He parked Sami's Corolla behind the shop and returned the keys.

Route 8 seemed to have less traffic than Coop remembered and he entered the outskirts of Karbala in less than forty-five minutes. It took him another half-hour dodging pushcarts and pickup trucks before reaching Ghazali's house.

Yesterday, when they searched the house, Coop had assigned the bedroom to Marco. While tossing and turning last night, Coop began to question if Marco had the experience to do a thorough job. He didn't think it would hurt to give it another look.

Coop opened the front door and wrinkled his nose as the putrid odor of human decay flooded his nostrils. He lurched back, slammed the door and sucked in a lungful of fresh air. When the smell disappeared, he took off his t-shirt and wrapped it around his nose and mouth before opening the door again. He went directly to the source. Ghazali was still propped up at the kitchen table and was stiff as a board.

Coop eyed the bedroom. It was disheveled and the bed looked like it hadn't been made in weeks. The only other piece of furniture was an eight-drawer dresser. The six large drawers were stuffed with unfolded underwear, socks and T-shirts, but the two small drawers were full of Ghazali's personal items.

One drawer contained Ghazali's wallet and cell phone. Coop sorted through the wallet; it contained a few U.S. twenty-dollar bills but it had no identification at all—no driver's license, no appointment cards, no credit cards. The cell phone was a mess. It looked as though it had been smashed with a hammer.

The other small drawer revealed an unorganized collection of clutter. Coop sifted through it. There was a Seiko watch, a couple of gold rings, and several pins that advertised Saddam's Iraq.

Under the pins was a pile of photos. Most were pictures of Ghazali posing with other people. There was one with Saddam, one with an older couple, another with a teenage boy, several with what appeared to be friends, and then one that caught Coop's eye. Ghazali was holding a large rifle apparently posing with another person, but the picture was torn in half and the other half was missing. Coop put it in his pocket.

A wave of nausea gripped Coop. The odor of death was getting to him. He went back to his car and tried to recall the route to the police station. After a missed turn or two, he pulled into the parking lot.

Coop spotted the same officer he had talked to the day before and approached his desk. The mustached man looked up from his computer. "It is the American with the gold badge. Did you find the man you were looking for?"

"Yeah, I found him." Coop sat down on a vacant chair. "But he had a bullet through his forehead."

"It does not cause me surprise."

"Why is that?" Coop asked.

"I am used to seeing men like him. Most of them ended up dead. They would cause us much trouble. It seemed like someone would always come to their rescue. Eventually, someone would come to kill them."

"Who came to this guy's rescue?"

The officer relit a half-smoked cigar that had burned out in an ashtray. "For many years it was one of Saddam's men." He picked at a tooth and spit into a brass bowl on the floor. "But then Saddam went on the run."

"Then who came to his rescue?"

"An American."

"An American? What American?"

"I do not know."

"Was he from the embassy?" Coop asked. The officer shrugged his shoulders.

"The Army, maybe?" The man hunched his shoulders again. Coop stood to leave. "You better collect that guy's body. It's getting stiff." He shook the officer's hand and started for the door.

The policeman lifted his finger. "Wait, wait, I remember something. The American ... he had a badge. A badge that looked sort of like yours."

Sixteen

Before Lara left the hotel, she told Zoe she would work on her tax problem as soon as she got back to the office. She told her to come by later in the day.

The assistant escorted Zoe into Lara's private office. Lara was wearing a new blue dress and a different assortment of jewelry. She stood and adjusted her horn-rimmed readers. "Ms. Rawlings, please, take a seat. I've been looking forward to your arrival."

The assistant took Zoe's coat and left the office. Zoe waited for the door to close behind her. "You look nice," she said.

Lara settled in behind Zoe and kissed the side of her neck. "So do you. I've been thinking about what you said this morning."

"And what have you been thinking?"

"I'm hoping you were being honest and last evening wasn't a one-night-stand."

Zoe eased away. "It doesn't have to be, but it's going to get complicated. You may not want a personal relationship with me."

Lara returned to her desk and fumbled around for her glasses. "How naïve of me. There's someone else back home?"

Zoe took a seat facing her. "No, it's something else."

Lara opened a folder labeled: Rawlings. "It's quite all right, you don't have to explain. I should know better than to mix business with pleasure. I apologize. Let us get back to your tax proposal and forget last night ever happened."

Zoe rose, strolled to the wet bar and picked up a decanter. "Is this Scotch or brandy?"

"Brandy. Why?"

She poured two glasses and handed one to Lara. "Look, Lara, I'm the one who should be apologizing. My name isn't Kate Rawlings, I'm not from Charleston and I don't need the proposal."

"I do not understand."

"My name is Zoe Fields, I'm from Washington D.C. and I was sent here by the United States government."

Lara felt dots of sweat moisten her armpits. "The U.S. government? Why? What...what is going on here?"

"You worked with Amacher on a couple of Middle East deals."

"Yes, I told you I occasionally do that. Why is this a problem?"

Zoe opened her briefcase and took out a large brown envelope. She slid it across the desk to Lara. "Swiss Commerce Bank handled several financial transactions for the sale of Iraqi art relics."

"I ask again. Why is this a problem?"

"Because it appears you and Amacher skimmed off a lot of Swiss Francs disguised as fees. Some of the buyers were Americans. A good chunk of that money should have gone to the U.S. government."

"So, last night...it was just an assignment for you?"

"It started out that way, but that obviously changed." Zoe pushed the envelope in Lara's direction. "Take a look. There's a lot of incriminating evidence in here. I can help you."

Lara opened the envelope and began sorting through the documents. She drank the last of her brandy and pushed the papers in Zoe's direction. She reached for her glass, but it was empty. "Amacher came to me, you know. He needed buyers for an art collection. I merely suggested some of my personal clients." She went to the bar and poured herself another drink. Her hand was trembling. "Oh, God, Kate—Zoe—I had nothing to do with these transactions. I will be ruined if my name is connected with them."

"Look, Lara, I like you very much and I can get you out of this mess, but you'll have to trust me. Can you do that?"

"Yes, I'll trust you, but how...?"

"You help me get some files off Amacher's computer and your name will disappear from these records."

"How could I possibly help? I have no idea how to get into Christophe's computer."

"Let me worry about that. All you have to do is call Amacher and get him out of his office at three-thirty this afternoon."

"That's it?"

"That's it."

Lara went to Zoe and took Zoe's hands in hers. "Thank you, thank you so much...Ka...Zoe. Were you serious then...about coming back to Zurich one day?"

"Yes, I was serious," Zoe said. She stuffed the papers back into her folder and got up to leave. "Three-thirty. Sharp."

Zoe entered Amacher's outer office and approached his receptionist. "I'd like to see Mr. Amacher. Tell him it's the American from the elevator."

The receptionist tapped the intercom. "An American woman is here to see you. She says she's from an elevator."

A loud laugh erupted through the speaker. "Wonderful. Give me a minute."

Zoe heard the response and took a seat. She glanced at her watch; it was 2:52. The office door opened and Amacher appeared with his million-Euro smile. He kissed the top of her hand. "What an unexpected pleasure."

"I hope I'm not intruding."

"Don't be silly. Come in."

Amacher led Zoe into his private office. There was a business desk, but the rest of the room looked like an art gallery—paintings covered every wall. He offered Zoe a seat and he settled into a leather chair behind his desk. "I'm flattered," he said.

"You said, 'don't hesitate.'"

"And I meant it. May I get you a drink or coffee or..."

"No. Thank you. I want to ask a favor."

"By all means."

Zoe shifted in her seat and hesitated. "This is...a...a little uncomfortable. I wouldn't want Lara to think that I...you know, went behind her back."

"All my conversations are confidential."

"I appreciate that. Lara mentioned that you're an expert in Middle East exports."

Amacher smirked. "Not just an expert. The leading expert in the country, and if I may, possibly all of Europe."

"That's what I heard. I have quite a bit of cash in the U.S. I'd like to invest in Middle Eastern relics."

"And Lara advised against it?"

"Yes."

"I understand. She's quite conservative. Do you have any particular relics in mind?'

"It's been almost a year since Saddam was executed. Do you have access to any of his personal items?"

"What sort of personal items?"

"You know, stuff from the palace or the family. Hard to get stuff."

"If I may ask, how much are you planning to invest?"

"A couple hundred thousand."

Amacher pushed the power button on his computer and began to stroke the mouse with two fingers. When the screen lit up, he tapped a few keys and waited for a file to appear. He opened the file and began scrolling. Zoe looked at her watch again. It was 3:26.

"I have access to several of Saddam's pieces, but I'm afraid nothing for two hundred," he said.

Zoe looked disappointed. "I see. I guess I could go as high as half a million. Is there anything in that range?"

He began tapping and entering, tapping and entering. The intercom buzzed. Amacher pushed a button on the phone pad. "I'm busy."

The voice from the speaker said, "I'm sorry Mr. Amacher, it's Ms. Graf. She says it can't wait."

He was visibly annoyed and talked into the speakerphone. "Lara, what is it? I'm with a client."

"Something has come up and we have to talk immediately."

"I'm afraid I don't have time right now."

"Then make time. Our friend from the auditor's office wants a meeting."

"I see. When?"

"He is on his way over. We have twenty minutes to...uh...review things."

"I'll be right up," Amacher said. He turned to Zoe. "Ms. Rawlings, this is quite rude, but I have to attend to this issue. It shouldn't take long."

"No problem."

He looked at his watch again. "Thank you. May I have a coffee brought in?'

"That's not necessary. Attend to your business; I'll be here when you get back."

Amacher gave a little bow and hurried out the door. Zoe moved quickly to the computer. A screen saver image of the Swiss Alps filled the screen. She tapped ENTER. The Alps disappeared and a folder labeled IRAQ appeared on the screen. Zoe checked the size; it was over eight hundred files.

She pulled a flash-drive from her purse and inserted it into the USB port. She selected ALL FILES and clicked DOWNLOAD. A task bar appeared: TIME REMAINING 16 MINUTES.

Zoe knew she couldn't make the process go any faster, so she killed time by perusing the art that plastered the walls. She had examined almost every picture, when abruptly she stopped and cocked her head. She could hear voices coming from the outer office. She heard the receptionist say, "Back so soon?" And she heard Amacher say, "Yes, false alarm."

Zoe checked the task bar again. It read: TIME REMAINING 5 MINUTES. She considered stopping it, but decided against it. She returned to the art.

Amacher opened the door and rushed in. "Ms. Rawlings. Again, please accept my apologies."

"None necessary. Your fabulous art has kept me entertained. Are they all originals?"

He couldn't resist. "Of course," he said, and began his guided tour. "Cezanne, 1905...Picasso, 1937...Pollack, 1950..."

Zoe's head slumped and she fell to the ground. Amacher kneeled and bent over her. "Ms. Rawlings. Ms. Rawlings, are you okay?"

She lifted her head and mumbled, "I need...need something with sugar."

Amacher rushed out of the room. Zoe jumped up and scrambled to the computer. The task bar read: TIME REMAINING 0 MINUTES. She yanked out the flash drive and pushed the computer sleep button. Amacher came running back into the office. "Thank God, you're on your feet. Here, eat this." He handed Zoe a pastry.

She gulped down the sweet. "I mishandled my insulin again. Perhaps we could discuss the relics another time."

Amacher put his arm around her waist. "Of course, my dear. I'll see you to a taxi."

Seventeen

Zoe's plane was scheduled to land in Baghdad at 2:20 p.m. As usual, Marco did the driving and Coop relaxed in the passenger seat. Traffic suddenly screeched to a halt. Coop lit a cigarette. Marco stuffed a couple of sticks of gum in his mouth and looked at his watch. "How are we doing on time?"

Coop checked his phone. "Plenty of time. How was downtown yesterday?"

"I never made it. That breakfast got to me and I spent all afternoon on the pot. Hey, did you get your personal stuff taken care of?"

"Yeah, everything went well." Coop pointed to the road. "Traffic's moving."

Marco cracked his gum a couple of times and put the car in gear. Coop looked his way. "God, I hate that."

"Sorry, man. I didn't know."

"It's okay, I'm just a little on edge—personal stuff. Sorry."

Traffic slowed again to a crawl and Marco was getting antsy. When he finally spotted the exit to the airport, he raced through the roundabout and screeched to a stop in front of Turkish Airlines. Zoe was next to the curb sitting on her suitcase. Coop rolled down his window. "Hey there, baby, lookin' for a ride?"

Zoe gave him the finger. "Not with a couple of creeps like you." Coop broke up laughing and got out of the car. Zoe picked up her suitcase. "Hey boss, how goes it?"

"We're making progress. How did it go for you?"

She held up the flash drive. Coop gave her a hug and tossed her suitcase into the trunk while she settled into the back seat. He got in the car and handed Marco an address.

Marco pulled into a parking spot near the Smoke Shop; Coop grabbed his laptop and motioned everyone out of the car. Zoe looked up and down the street and then at Coop. "Why here?" she asked.

"Our rooms are bugged. It's safer here."

Coop led the others into the shop. The bodyguard gave him a familiar nod and Sami pulled his head from the newspaper. "Mr. Coop, back so soon?"

He handed Sami several bills. "We need the back room for a couple of hours."

Sami apparently approved of the donation and pointed to several strings of hanging beads that separated the shop from the back room. Coop spread the beads and the group disappeared behind them.

Zoe looked around. The couch was old and badly stained—probably a sponge for everything spilled on it over the last twenty years. There were also a coffee table marked with cigarette burns and two unmatching chairs with stuffing popping out. She took a whiff of the air and pinched her nose. "Jeez, it stinks in here. This is the best place you could find?"

Coop gave her a dismissive gesture. "Trust me. The only bugs in here are crawling. Got that flash drive?" Zoe handed Coop the drive and he snapped it into his laptop. The three of them huddled up to view the screen.

There were over eight hundred files in Amacher's IRAQ folder, but Coop was only interested in the ones from 2006 and 2007. He began opening them.

"What are we looking for?" Marco asked.

Coop didn't take his eyes off the screen. "Something big. We'll know it when we see it." He kept opening files, studying them and closing them. Open...study...close...it went on for two and a half hours.

"Amacher skimmed a hunk of dough from every one of these deals," Zoe said.

"Yeah, but that's not really our mission, is it?" Open...study... close...and then a message appeared on one file: PASSWORD REQUIRED. Coop tried again, but he couldn't get past the message.

"What d'ya think?" Marco said.

"Could be it." Coop looked at Zoe. "Did you get any passwords?"

Zoe looked surprised. "I didn't think we needed any. The folder was open."

"For some reason he chose to put an extra security layer on this file," Coop said.

She looked disappointed. "Can it be hacked?"

Coop closed his laptop and removed the flash drive. "I think so. I have a guy."

~ * ~

Gordon married Fran's sister, Myra, a couple of years after Coop and Fran were married. They were both over forty; no children were ever in the picture. Gordon's kids were his electronics and their home was the 3rd floor of the Agency building. The room in which he worked was packed with computers, scanners, printers, and a bunch of equipment that only a computer nerd could identify. Gordon's phone lit up with an I.D. and he flipped it open. "Coop? Is that you?"

"Hey, Gordon. How's my favorite brother-in-law?"

"I'm fine. Fran said you went back to Iraq last week. Are you home now?'

"No, I'm still in Baghdad."

"So, let me guess. You need a favor."

"Well...yeah, I do. I have to get into a file that's password protected. Think you can do it?"

"Probably. How fast do you need it?"

"Is yesterday too soon?"

"E-mail it to me. I'll see what I can do."

"Great, but Gordon...no one else at the Agency can know about this."

"Okay, I get it. A James Bond special."

Eighteen

It was 5:00 a.m. and the only people in the embassy garage were Coop's team: Zoe, Marco, and Ahmad. They huddled next to a mud-splattered SUV equipped with large bumpers and mirrored glass. The elevator door opened and Coop strolled into the garage. "Nothin' like a tour of the countryside," he said. "Let's do it."

Everyone piled into the SUV. Ahmad was the only one who had been to Tikrit; it was a given he would take the driver's seat. Coop again rode shotgun. Zoe and Marco spread out in the back seats. The first fifty kilometers north of Baghdad were uneventful and they made good time until Ahmad spotted activity ahead and slowed down. A half-dozen armed men in uniforms were blocking the highway; one holding a semi-automatic signaled the SUV to stop. Coop looked at Ahmad. "It's okay, they're Iraqi military," Ahmad said.

Ahmad brought the vehicle to a stop and rolled down the window as the ranking officer approached them. Coop took out his credentials, leaned over Ahmad and handed them to the soldier. The captain inspected the papers and handed them back through the open window. "Where will you be going today?"

"Tikrit," Coop said.

"Be careful. There are many insurgents on this road."

Coop put the documents back in his pocket. "Thanks, we'll keep our eyes open."

Ahmad closed the window, threw the vehicle back into gear and ran it up to 120 kph. The chatter in the car disappeared as Zoe and Marco fell asleep. Coop silently surveyed the landscape and Ahmad kept his eyes on the road. It took another hour before a sign reading, TIKRIT 2 KM, came into view. From a distance, Saddam's home town, nestled against the west bank of the Tigris river, looked charming, but as they got a closer, the ravages of war showed everywhere. Buildings were bombed-out, streets were torn apart and most of the homes were in disrepair. Ahmad slowed the SUV and Coop handed him an address. "Hopefully the family still lives here."

They entered a neighborhood that appeared to have been spared from most of the destruction. Ahmad spotted the address Coop had given him and pulled to a stop in front of a small, but well-kept house. Coop turned to Zoe. "This could be touchy; we don't want to intimidate her. You and Ahmad go. Marco and I will stay here."

Zoe knocked on the front door. After a prolonged wait, a woman opened it. She wore a scarf over her head, but her face was exposed. Her eyes radiated sadness and the wrinkles forming on her cheeks and forehead revealed a person who looked older than her years. She was closely flanked by her teenage son and her younger daughter. Zoe spoke to her through Ahmad's translation. "Mrs. Mustafa? I'm here from the American Embassy."

The woman remained stoic, while the teenage boy moved closer and clasped his mother's hand. The young girl held tightly to her mother's dress—tears welling in her eyes. The woman didn't speak, but Zoe was sure they had the right house. Zoe prompted Ahmad what to say. "I heard about your husband. I'm very sorry. May I speak to you?"

The woman became angry and raised her voice. Ahmad turned to Zoe. "She wants to know what this is about."

"Tell her we understand her husband knew Saddam." Mrs. Mustafa heard Saddam's name and tried to close the door, but Zoe held her hand against it. She said to Ahmad, "Tell her we're not here to punish anyone. We just need a little information."

"She says she has no information."

"Tell her that her husband said he knew where Saddam hid his gold."

"She says it got her husband killed."

"Tell her I understand, but it's safe now. Saddam is gone. Tell her there's a reward. Tell her if she can lead us to the gold, she'll get lots of money."

The woman's anger rose as she spoke with Ahmad. He turned to Zoe. "She says she wants nothing to do with it. She wants nothing to do with you. She says she just wants you to go away."

Mrs. Mustafa waited until the translation was finished before she pushed the children inside the house and slammed the door.

Ahmad and Zoe trudged backed to the car and got in. Coop looked at his watch. "That was quick."

Zoe shook her head. "She's scared shitless."

"Maybe I should give it a try."

"Don't bother, it's useless. Let's get out of here."

Coop gave the go-ahead to Ahmad and he started the car, but before he could put it into gear there was a tapping on the side glass. Coop lowered the window. Mustafa's son, a boy trying to be man before his time, was looking in. "How much the reward?" he asked.

"Twenty-thousand dollars," Coop said.

"My mother? She will get all of it?"

"If you help us find the gold."

"Do you promise?"

He hesitated for a moment, remembering his track record for promises wasn't very good lately. "Yeah, I promise."

"Okay, I take you to the warehouse."

Ahmad followed the boy's directions, which shortly led them out of the city limits and on to the only highway heading west. A couple of miles beyond the city the boy leaned forward from the back seat and pointed to a dirt road that was hardly noticeable to anyone but him. "We turn," he said. Ahmad took a right and within a hundred yards they were in what appeared to be the middle of nowhere.

The landscape was desolate and the dirt road was gouged with ruts. They bounced along for a quarter of a mile before the boy leaned forward again and pointed to a structure situated fifty yards off the road. Ahmad acknowledged and took a left onto a beat-up pathway.

The warehouse didn't look like a warehouse; it looked more like an old wood barn. It probably had paint on it at one time, but the weather had taken its toll. It was bleached by the sun and pitted by the blowing sand.

Everyone piled out of the car and approached two swinging doors held together by a lock and chain. Coop took Marco with him to do reconnaissance around back while the others waited by the doors. After a full circle of the barn, Coop and Marco rejoined the group and reported there were no windows or doors other than the ones in front of them.

Zoe pointed to the chain and lock. "Well, I guess we go through here then."

Coop turned to Marco. "Okay, big guy, put that weight to good use."

Marco wound up and jammed the heel of his right shoe against one of the doors. The old wood cracked. He gave it another shot. This time it fractured and a section fell to the ground along with the lock and the chain. Coop gave Marco a congratulatory pat on the back. "Hey buddy, it's nice having you around."

Coop led the way as the group entered the barn. Slivers of sunlight showed through the warped wood siding, but it was still too dark to make anything out. They turned on their flashlights; the beams bounced off the walls and ceiling of the hollow structure as they searched for signs of the gold.

Cobwebs laced the corners and hung from the rafters. The floor, which appeared to be cement, was layered with dust and an assortment of discarded nails, screws, and food wrappers. The only furniture in the building were two large workbenches and a dilapidated desk. There were no crates, no barrels, and to everyone's despair, no gold.

The agents were disappointed, but the boy could barely hold back his tears. Coop put an arm around his shoulder. "Are you sure this is the place?"

The boy wiped his nose with his shirt sleeve. "I am sure. My father bring me here when the barrels, they were delivered. There were many men with guns. This warehouse was full with barrels." He began to sob. "My mother will not get the money."

"Hey, it's okay." Coop patted the boy's back. You can still help us. And don't worry...we'll get some money to your mom."

Coop led the group back outside where he bent down and ran his hand over the ruts in the dirt. "Something heavy made these." He turned to the boy. "You said you saw trucks. What kind of trucks? Big trucks, little trucks? What kind of trucks?"

"I don't know. Maybe big. Maybe not too big."

"Were they vans? Panel trucks?"

The boy started to cry again. "I don't know about trucks."

Zoe came to him and gave him a big hug. "It's okay, it's okay. Is there anything you can remember about the trucks?"

The boy hugged Zoe back. "I don't remember the trucks...but...but I can take you to the company that owns them." Zoe kissed his forehead.

The SUV bounced along the road heading back to the highway. Zoe stretched out in the back seat and propped her feet on top of the console next to Coop. He pushed them away. "Come on, Zoe, move those." Coop looked at his hand. "Whoa, what's all this weird stuff on your shoes?"

Zoe gazed at her sneakers. They were covered in a brownish-yellow powder. "I have no idea."

Everyone else in the car examined their shoes. They were all covered with the same powder. Coop rubbed some of the dust between his thumb and forefinger, sniffed it and put a dab on his tongue. "Ugh." He made a face and wiped his fingers on his jeans.

The boy directed Ahmad to the trucking company parking lot. It was filled with a variety of trucks, but they all had one thing in common. They displayed the same logo—a large lion's head. There were no buildings on the property; the only structure even resembling an office was an old beat-up trailer.

Just in case he needed an interpreter, Coop took Ahmad with him into the trailer. It was a mess. Boxes, oil cans, and truck parts were piled everywhere. A small space was carved out for a desk where the owner, an unshaven man with grease-covered hands, was sitting.

"Speak English?" Coop asked.

The owner spat on the floor. "Everybody does... now."

Coop opened his wallet and flashed his badge. The owner waved it off. "You can put that away. It don't scare me."

He closed the wallet. "How's your memory?"

"Sometimes good. Sometimes not so good."

Coop took out a hundred-dollar bill and dropped it on the desk. "I need some information."

"And my kids...they need shoes."

He dropped another hundred on the desk. "For shoes."

"Winter clothes...they need winter clothes."

Coop set down another bill. "For clothes."

"They also need..."

Coop scooped up the cash and nudged Ahmad toward the door. "Forget it," he said.

The owner stood and held his hands in the air. "Wait, wait. What do you want to know?"

Coop put the money back on the desk. "There's an old barn west of town, 'bout two miles off the main road. You know it?"

"Yes, I know this place. I deliver cargo there."

"Cargo? What kind of cargo?"

"Barrels. Hundreds of barrels. Take five of my trucks."

"Barrels of what?"

"I only pick up and deliver. I don't look in barrels, but whatever was inside was heavy—very heavy."

The owner reached for the bills, but Coop put his hand back on them. "You said you delivered cargo to the barn. Did you ever see it after that?"

"A year later I pick it up again."

"Where did you take it that time?" Coop asked.

"Istanbul...the airport...Burma Airlines."

"When? Exactly?"

The owner ran his greasy finger across the calendar. "September four."

"Who paid you?

"Small gangster from Baghdad—big cigar." He pointed to the front of his mouth. "And shiny gold tooth right here."

Coop took his hand off the bills. "Hope the kids stay warm this winter." He and Ahmad walked out of the trailer. The owner picked up his cell phone.

Nineteen

Ahmad looked to the west; the sun was close to the horizon. He pressed down on the accelerator and pushed the speed envelope to 150 kph. The only sounds inside the car were coming from the back seats where Marco and Zoe were passed out and sawing logs.

A half hour after leaving Tikrit, Ahmad turned to Coop. "There's no way we'll make it back before dark."

"Think it'll be a problem?"

"I hope not."

The sun set twenty minutes later. It appeared they were the only vehicle on the highway, so Ahmad clicked on the high beams and increased their speed to 160 kph. All went well until the SUV rounded a forty-five-degree curve. Fifty yards ahead was a wooden barricade with four armed men, dressed in fatigues and sandals, standing in front of it. Another half a dozen leaned against a truck, smoking. Coop looked at Ahmad. "What d'ya think?"

"Not good."

Coop turned toward the back seat. "Hey, wake up—trouble." Zoe and Marco snapped to attention. The agents took out their weapons and Coop handed one to Ahmad. "Okay, we stop, but under no circumstance do we get out of this vehicle. Whatever it takes, we do not get out."

Ahmad brought the SUV to a halt a few feet short of the barricade. The mirrored windows allowed the agents to see out, but the guerillas couldn't see in. Two of the armed men jumped on the right running board—the other two on the left. They tried to look into the vehicle, but the mirrored glass didn't allow it. The man next to the driver's door banged the butt of his rifle against the window. "Open thees door."

Ahmad looked at Coop. Coop held his thumb and index finger an inch apart. Ahmad opened the window a crack. "What do you want?"

The armed man spoke into the opening. "Everyone will get out."

"We're on government business. We're not carrying any money," Ahmad said.

The man hammered the rifle butt against the window again. This time it cracked. "Out...now."

Coop looked around. The entire team had their pistols in the ready position—two pointed left and two pointed right. Coop held up three fingers and began counting down. When the last finger disappeared into his fist, all four weapons fired simultaneously. The windows exploded and blood sprayed over the sides of the car as the men tumbled to the ground. Ahmad jammed the gas pedal to the floor. The SUV leaped forward and smashed through the barricade, its over-sized bumper sending wood flying into the air. The men loitering next to the truck grabbed their rifles and began firing. The rear window of the SUV shattered as it accelerated out of sight.

"Zoe's been hit," Marco yelled.

Blood was pulsating through Zoe's shirt. Ahmad pushed harder on the gas pedal and the speedometer jumped to 178 kph. Coop snapped off his seatbelt, crawled over the console and tumbled into the back seats. Zoe had been shot in the left arm just above the elbow and was losing a lot of blood. They reclined the seat and laid her out in the prone position. Marco already had Zoe's left sleeve ripped off her shirt and he was putting pressure on the wound. Coop put his hand on Zoe's forehead. She felt cold and clammy. "How're you doing?" he asked.

"A little light-headed."

Coop yelled at Ahmad. "How long?"

He glanced at his speedometer and did the math. "Forty minutes."

Coop looked at Zoe. "You hear that?"

"Yeah, I'm good."

Coop took off his belt and pulled it tight around Zoe's arm just below the shoulder. The bleeding slowed. Marco used what was left of Zoe's shirt sleeve and wrapped it firmly around the wound. Air was rushing in through the broken windows. Zoe began to shiver. Both men stripped off their jackets, draped them over her and leaned in close to share their body heat.

They called ahead and the emergency room doctors were waiting when Ahmad screeched to a stop. They put Zoe on a gurney and wheeled her into the hospital. Coop looked at Ahmad and Marco. "You guys did so good. Get some rest. I'll make sure she's okay."

Marco clutched Coop's hand and gave him a one-handed bear hug with the other. "So did you, boss."

Coop was drowning in coffee by the time the doctor came into the waiting room. "Agent Cooper?" Coop nodded. The doctor handed Coop his belt. "Your tourniquet did the job. The bullet was a through and through; luckily it missed the brachial artery. The smaller vessel that was hit was already clotted by the time we got in there."

"That's good news. Is she going to be laid up for a while?"

"Not really. We'll keep her here overnight...a sling for a week and she's good to go."

"Can I see her?" Coop asked.

"Go on in. She's been asking for you."

He tapped lightly on the door and stepped into the room. Zoe had an IV in her right arm and a taped dressing on her left. Her eyes were closed. He leaned up next to her. "You awake?" he whispered.

Zoe lids opened. "Yeah, sorta."

"How are you feeling?"

"I'm on morphine. I'm feeling great."

"I'm sorry, Zoe.'

"For what?"

"For almost getting you killed."

"Come on, the job is what gets us killed."

"Is it?" Coop spent a moment in thought. "Yeah, I guess you're right, but I'm just tired of emergency rooms."

Zoe was working hard to keep her eyes open..."I understa..." she drifted off. Coop pulled a leather chair from the corner, curled up and fell asleep.

He woke with a start; a nurse was taking Zoe's vitals. Zoe saw Coop's head jerk and she leaned toward him. "Hey, sleepy, I didn't want to wake you." Coop looked at his watch. It was five-fifteen in the morning. The nurse finished her duties and slipped out of the room. Coop had a far-away look.

"Are you going to let me in?" Zoe asked.

Coop snapped out of his trance. "Sure, I dreamt about the night you and I met."

"In Poland?"

"Yeah, you were undercover. I had no idea we were on the same team and..."

"...and you thought you were going to bed with a Russian spy."

He laughed. "I figured I could wait until morning before I shoot you."

"Why didn't you?"

"I was young. I thought I was in love with you."

"Were you?"

He thought about it. "Yeah, I probably was."

They both let the words settle for a few minutes before Zoe said, "What's bothering you, Coop?"

"Am I that easy to read?"

"Back in D.C. you said things weren't going well with the family."

He winced. "I let Josh down. I promised him I wouldn't go away again."

"Have you called him?"

"I got so caught up in this thing, I forgot. Fran called me yesterday...and she was pissed."

"You can patch it up."

"I've been patching it up for ten years. I'm not sure it will work anymore."

"Call Josh right now."

Coop looked at his watch. "It's too late back there."

"He's still up. It's only nine-fifteen in D.C. Go, go into the hall. Call him."

Coop took his cell from his pocket and stared at it for a moment or two. He checked his watch again and dragged himself to the door. He looked back. Zoe was nodding.

Josh answered on the first ring. "Hi, Dad."

"Hey, buddy. How you doin?"

"Fine."

"School good?"

"Yeah."

"Basketball?"

"It's good."

"That's good."

Josh paused. "Is anyone shooting at you?" He asked.

"No, I'm at a desk all day."

"When are you coming home?"

Coop hesitated. "Soon."

"What does that mean—soon?"

"It means I'm trying as hard as I can to get home."

"I miss you, Dad."

"I miss you too. I'm going to make it up to you. I prom...uh...I will."

"Okay, Mom wants to talk to you."

Fran took the phone from Josh and walked into the kitchen. "What did you tell Josh?"

"That I'd be home soon."

"And will you?"

"I hope so."

"Coop...I...I saw a lawyer this morning."

Coop was silent. He looked in his pocket for a cigarette, then remembered he was in a hospital. "Fran, please, please don't do this."

"What do you want me to do? Keep lying to Josh? Keep telling him his dad will be home in a few days until he doesn't have a dad anymore?"

"I'll make this my last assignment. I'll take early retirement."

"No, you won't. You know you won't." Her voice cracked. "I can't let you do this to him any longer. When, if ever you get back, don't plan on living here. I just can't take this anymore."

"Fran...Fran?" The line was dead.

Coop stepped back into Zoe's room. "How'd it go?" she asked.

He forced a weary smile. "Fine. Yeah, just fine."

Twenty

Coop slammed the door and stomped into the Smoke Shop. The bodyguard barely looked up. Sami raised his eyebrows. "Mr. Coop, welcome back."

Coop approached the counter, grabbed Sami by the front of his shirt and pulled him close enough to smell the garlic on his breath. "You fuckin' asshole." The bodyguard jumped to his feet and started toward Coop. Coop dropped Sami and reached for his pistol. "Sit down, Tiny, or I'll blow your head off." Sami motioned the big guy back to his seat.

"You do not look happy my friend," Sami said.

"You noticed."

"Please, come to my private office. We talk."

Sami led Coop into a room just large enough to fit a card table and two chairs. The table was stacked with papers and those that didn't make it to the table were piled in the corner. Sami used his handkerchief to dust off one of the chairs and bowed to Coop, signaling him to sit.

"So, Mr. Coop. What did I do to make you so angry?"

"We've given you a pass to run your operation out of Baghdad, but I just found out you did a big business deal in Tikrit."

"I make many trips to Tikrit. My brother lives there. If I can do a little business when I am there, why would this make you unhappy?"

"You arranged for a truck shipment from Tikrit to Istanbul."

"Mr. Coop, Mr. Coop, you know how I make my living. I do favors for people and people pay me for the favors."

"Who paid you for this favor?"

"Surely you know my business relies on privacy. No privacy, no business. So, please..." Sami stood and started for the door.

Coop shoved him back in his chair. "And surely you know who I work for."

Sami's condescending attitude disappeared. "Of course, I do."

"Then how long do you think it will take me to put your favor business out of business?'

Sami began to perspire. "Mr. Coop, plea..."

"Who paid you?"

Sami used the dusty handkerchief to wipe his forehead. "The man was a courier. He came to the shop with ten thousand dollars and directions to a place outside Tikrit. All I do is arrange to get the stuff from an old barn to the airport in Istanbul."

"This courier, where was he from?"

"I don't know for sure, but he spoke English with a slight Persian accent."

"Iranian?"

Sami lifted his eyebrows. "Maybe."

Twenty-one

The flight from Baghdad to Istanbul took a little over three hours, but the airport was such a mess the walk from the plane to the front of the terminal ate up another forty minutes. The Divan Istanbul Hotel, where Coop booked three rooms, was only four miles from the airport and had its own shuttle. He told Zoe and Marco to grab it and check in. He'd join them later.

Coop headed in the opposite direction where he spotted a directory for the airline business offices. He ran his finger down the list. Fourth floor: Turkish Airlines, EgyptAir, Asiana Airlines, Burma Airlines. He hopped in the elevator.

When the doors opened, Coop was looking straight across the hall at the Burma Airlines office. He tucked his shirt into his khakis and went inside. The reception area displayed the airline logo on the front wall—a world globe with the name *Burma Air* in the center. The receptionist straightened up in her chair. "May I help you?"

Coop showed his badge. "I need to talk to whoever's in charge."

"That would be Mr. Saraaf. Please take a seat and I'll see if he's available."

Coop picked up a copy of the *Burma Air Magazine.* The cover featured the *BA* logo along with the slogan, "Gateway to Asia." The stories inside were devoted to the airline's major destinations: Bangkok, Kuala Lumpur, Singapore, Hong Kong, and Istanbul. Coop wasn't interested in the airlines' PR program and set the journal back on the table.

The receptionist interrupted his boredom. "Mr. Cooper, I'll show you in now." She seated him facing a large desk and told him it wouldn't be long.

Coop eyeballed Saraaf's desk. Snooping—anytime and anywhere—was a major part of Coop's job description. He stood and did a quick check of the door. No one appeared to be in a hurry to join him, so he began sorting through the items on the desk. There was a small pile of papers. He flipped through them, but they were just vendor contracts—not of any interest to him. A dozen letters were held down by a paperweight—routine stuff just waiting for a signature. A couple of paperbacks were stacked near the edge of the desk. Coop picked one up. He couldn't read the title because it was written in Arabic, but it had an interesting cover; an island surrounded by sparkling turquoise water. Before Coop could leaf through it, an Indian gentleman wearing a tailored blue suit and a matching blue tie entered the office. Coop stood and tossed the book back on the desk.

"Mr. Cooper...Deepak Saraaf." The man thrust out his hand.

"A pleasure," Coop said, sitting down after Saraaf settled behind his desk.

Saraaf folded his hands. "I must say, I'm quite surprised your government has sent yet another department head to investigate the disappearance of flight five-seven-one. Since the plane went missing two weeks ago, I have shared everything I know with your country."

"I'm not here about the missing plane."

"Really. Then why..."

"I'm tracking some cargo that was delivered to your shipping dock."

"I'm afraid that's not something I deal with. I suggest you talk to our freight manager."

"I was hoping you could speed up the process."

"I'm a busy man, Mr. Cooper."

"So am I, Mr. Saraaf."

Saraaf stared at Coop. Coop stared back. Saraaf looked at his desktop and noticed the paperback was out of place. He dropped it into a drawer and said, "Very well. What can you tell me about the shipment?"

"It was from Iraq and it was big."

Saraaf smirked. "We handle many big shipments from Iraq. I'm afraid I'll need more than that."

"Okay. It was brought to your docks by five two-ton trucks. They left Tikrit on September fourth. I'm guessing they got to your dock around the seventh or eighth. How 'bout you run that by your freight manager?"

Saraaf didn't bother to hide his annoyance. He picked up the phone, tapped a couple numbers and began conversing rapidly in Turkish. Coop had no idea what was being said; only the word Tikrit was recognizable.

"*Evet, evet*, yes, yes, thank you, Kasim." Saraaf hung up and looked at Coop. "My manager said he has no record of any shipment that large. Perhaps it was another airline."

"I don't think so."

"Well, my freight manager thinks so."

"Well, maybe you need a new freight manager."

Saraaf stood up. "I'm sorry Mr. Cooper, I've done all I can do."

"You haven't done squat."

"Is there anything else?" Saraaf asked.

Coop stood. "No, sorry to take up your valuable time." He slammed the door behind him.

He pushed the elevator button and looked at the digital display. The elevator was still in the basement. While he waited for it to come up, a guy in an airport security uniform passed by. "Hey," Coop yelled.

The man turned and said something in Turkish, or Arabic, or some other language that Coop didn't understand. "English?" Coop said.

"Do you need help, sir?"

"Yeah, I need to see some airport security tapes. Who should I talk to?"

"That would be Chief Fahri. His office is one floor down." Coop waited for the elevator and pushed the button for the third floor.

Coop showed his badge to the attendant and asked to see the chief. He was told to take a seat, but the only one available was next to a wide-eyed guy who kept yelling something about a missing piece of luggage. Every time he appeared under control, he would start ranting and raving all over again. Coop passed on the seat and leaned against the wall a safe distance away.

The door to the inner office opened and a well-built man sporting a thick black mustache and a shaved head looked out. "Mr. Cooper?"

He straightened up and hustled through the door just in time to avoid another luggage tirade. "Sounds like he really misses that suitcase," Coop said.

Chief Fahri glanced at the loudmouth and laughed, "Oh, him? He's never been on an airplane. He comes here for the attention. So, Mr. Cooper, I understand you are a U.S. agent."

Coop showed his credentials. "Chief, do you have security cameras on your loading docks?"

"Of course. I assume you want to see one of the recordings."

"Actually, I need to see a lot of them; all the Burma Air loading docks for September seventh and eighth."

The chief stroked his mustache, "That's a lot of footage."

"I've got time."

The chief led Coop to a large room that looked a lot like an air traffic control facility. The lights were dim and dozens of screens, grouped in threes, lined the walls with one inspector assigned to each group. A couple of empty desks with twenty-four-inch iMacs were set against the rear wall. The chief motioned Coop to one of them and powered it up. "I'll give you access, but keep in mind that some of the recordings may be locked."

"Why's that?"

"Flight five-seven-one. It went missing on the eighth."

"Okay, show me what you got."

The chief tapped a few keys until a long list of Burma Air flights appeared on the screen. He typed 9/7/2007 – 9/8/2007. The list got shorter, but still contained at least fifty flights. "Good luck," the chief said. "I'll check on you later."

Burma Air's first flight on September 7th was at 1:47 a.m.; the last one on September 8th was at 11:56 p.m. Coop started through the black and white footage. It was slow going to view every plane and every truck. He speeded up the process—fast forward...pause... fast forward...pause—but every recording looked the same. Forklifts moved back and forth between trucks and portable elevators that lifted cartons and containers into the waiting cargo holds of the airliners... fast forward...pause...fast forward...pause.

The security chief walked up behind Coop. "It's been almost four hours. Have you found what you are looking for?"

Coop rubbed his eyes. "No, maybe I have the wrong days."

The chief pulled up a chair and slid the keyboard in front of him. "So, tell me exactly what you are looking for."

"Five big trucks, all with a lion's head logo on their side panels."

The chief was fast. It only took him a minute or two for each flight. Coop needed a break. "Be right back. I'm going to hit the head," Coop said. The chief acknowledged but didn't look up.

He was only a few steps away when the chief raised his voice. "There. There they are."

Coop hurried back and looked at the frozen screen. "I see trucks unloading but they don't have the logos."

The chief pointed to the screen. "No, no. Not at the loading dock... outside the gate. Look, look here at the top of the screen. Those trucks are on their way to a different dock."

Coop squinted at the frozen image. It captured several trucks passing by the gate. They all had a logo of a lion's head. Coop patted the chief on the shoulder. "That's great. Can we run the next recording? See which flight they went to?"

The chief tapped a couple of keys. "Oh, oh."

"What?"

The chief frowned. "It's locked."

Twenty-two

Hertz was everywhere and the Istanbul airport was no exception. Coop still had a little cash left in his budget; he rented a full size.

The sign for the hotel appeared through the windshield at the same time the buzz sounded on Coop's phone. He looked at the ID and picked it up. "Gordon?"

"Hey, Coop, I got into that file."

"Did you find anything?"

"Yeah, some good stuff. Someone sold a lot of goods from Iraq to someone else for a lot of cash."

"You mean cash, cash?"

"Yep, ten million—all green."

"When?"

"A down payment of a million was made on September first. It looks like the rest isn't due for thirty days."

Coop did the math; it wasn't rocket science. "That's October first, so I still have ten days before the trail goes cold."

"It looks that way."

"Where's the exchange taking place?"

"Wherever the goods ended up."

"And where's that?"

"I have no idea. That's for you to find out."

"I suppose there's no name for the buyer or seller."

"You suppose right, but the transaction was handled by a bank in Zurich."

"Let me guess, the Swiss Commerce Bank?"

"Bingo," Gordon said. "Look, there are some other details. I'll put a password on the file and e-mail it to you. Do you remember Fran's birthday?"

Coop laughed. "I better or I'm in deep shit."

"Okay, check your inbox."

"Thanks, great job. Hey, Gordon, I have one more favor to ask. Have you ever hacked into a company's security recordings?"

"Sure, we do it all the time."

"I need you to check the footage from the flight five-seven-one loading dock." Gordon didn't answer. "Gordon, are you still there?" Coop asked.

"I'm here. Flight five-seven-one? Are you talking about Burma Airlines flight five-seven-one?"

"Yeah, that one."

"You must be kidding. They'll hang me by the balls."

"Look, you don't have to download anything. I just need to know if five trucks with a lion's head logo put cargo on that plane."

"Hey, tomorrow's Saturday."

"Just a look—a peek. It's important."

Gordon hesitated. "Damn it, Coop, I'm only five years away from retirement."

"Come on, Gordon, I'm not asking you to hack the president's e-mail or do anything illegal, just look for some trucks."

"Okay. Okay, I'll do it, but after this one, find yourself a new guy."

Twenty-three

The Divan Istanbul wasn't a fancy hotel, but it did have a great bar. Zoe and Marco were settled into the red velour bench-seats of a booth located in the back of the room, well away from the cigar smokers. Coop spotted them and slipped in next to Zoe. She slid a glass in front of him. "Scotch, I thought you might need it. Food's on the way."

He took a generous gulp. "Thanks, I do."

Small talk relating to the hard beds, the crappy showers and the pull-chain toilets took up the next five minutes until Zoe addressed the elephant in the room. "So, where was the gold shipped?"

Coop drained his glass. "I don't know for sure, but I'm thinking it was on flight five-seven-one."

Marco lifted his eyebrows. "No, that can't be. Are you sure?"

"Not a hundred percent, but my guy is checking it out in the morning."

"Guy? What guy?" Marco asked.

Before Coop could answer, a waitress approached the booth and began unloading food onto the table. One platter had fried eggplants with some sort of minced meat, onions, and parsley, and the other was a baked dough wrapped around meat and tomatoes with spices sprinkled on top. They passed the platter around and everyone loaded their plates. Marco washed it down with a gulp of beer. "So, what guy?" he asked again.

"I've got a sleeper in the Agency," Coop said.

"Really? Who?"

"Just a guy."

"What's the big secret? You can't tell us who it is?"

"I can. I just don't want to."

Marco set down his fork and turned to Zoe. "What is this? I thought we were a team."

"If Coop wanted us to know, he'd tell us. It's not that big a deal."

Marco pursed his lips and went back to his food, refusing to make eye contact with either Zoe or Coop. Coop stared at him. "My brother-in-law, okay? He's the head of the tech department. Is little Marco feeling better now?"

"I just..."

"Just keep it to yourself," Coop said.

"So, if it turns out the gold was on flight five-seven-one, is our mission over?" Zoe asked.

Coop thought about it. "Maybe. Maybe not."

"What do mean, maybe not?" Marco asked.

"Where's the plane?" Coop said.

"Where? How about the bottom of the ocean?"

Coop spotted the waitress and raised his glass in the air. She waved back and headed to the bar. "Look, not a single piece of the missing plane has been discovered. I'm just saying let's dig around a little more."

"Dig? Investigators have been digging for almost two weeks. What are we going to find that they didn't?"

"That's kinda the point, isn't it? They didn't find anything."

"The deputy director will blow a fuse if this turns out to be a wild goose chase."

"Look, Marco, Randy doesn't have to know. Not yet anyway."

"Is that proper protocol?"

Coop yanked Marco's plate away from him. "You know what? Just when I was getting to like you, you're becoming a pain in the ass."

Marco's face flushed. "Sorry...sorry for trying to do my job." He slid out of the booth and stormed out of the room.

Zoe looked at Coop and laughed. "What was that about?"

"No idea, but I don't have time for temper tantrums." Coop reached into his pocket and pulled out several folded sheets of paper. He dropped them on the table in front of Zoe and patted out the creases. "I got these from the airport security chief."

Zoe skimmed through the data. "The passenger manifest for flight five-seven-one?"

"Yeah, it's interesting. The plane had room for almost two hundred passengers, but only thirty-five were on board."

"So?"

"I checked it out. Flight five-seven-one went from Istanbul to Kuala Lumpur and it only went twice a week. It was always over-booked."

"Who knows? Maybe it was bad weather...or, a religious holiday...or, I don't know. There could be a dozen reasons."

The waitress arrived with a glass of Scotch and two Heinekens. She realized Marco was gone and took one glass back with her. Coop took a sip of the Scotch and handed Zoe another piece of paper. "I googled every name; eighteen had fancy scientific degrees."

"What d'ya mean scientific?"

"You know, like high tech stuff like geothermal physics and nuclear physics and all kinds of engineering. That kind of stuff."

"Honestly Coop, I'm not sure where you're going with this."

"I'm not sure either. It's just...I don't know...hard to believe."

Zoe wrinkled her brow. "What? That scientists ride on airplanes?"

"That so many were on board and no one even mentioned it. Throw in the possibility that the gold may have been on the plane too and it's just..."

"Just what?"

"Just hard to believe it's on the bottom of the ocean."

"So, what are you thinking?"

"Flight five-seven-one had a pilot. I'm thinking tomorrow we talk to his wife."

Coop signed his name to the bill and as soon as he checked into his room he plugged in his laptop. The email from Gordon was waiting. He downloaded the attachment, typed in Fran's date of birth and sifted through the file while making mental notes. When he had the contents memorized, he transferred the file to a flash drive and called Zoe's room. "Are you decent? I have something I want to show you."

"I just got out of the shower. Give me five minutes."

He gave her an extra ten before he knocked on her door and handed over the flash drive. "It looks like your Swiss banker friend is in deeper than you thought." He took a ballpoint from his pocket and wrote 9-15-70 on the back of her hand. "The password. Wash it off after you open the file."

As soon as Coop headed back to his room, Zoe placed the flash drive into her computer and typed in the password. She re-read the e-mail twice to make sure she wasn't mistaken and when she was sure she wasn't, she reached for her phone and flipped through her address book until she found the number for the Swiss Commerce Bank. After reintroducing herself to the receptionist as Kate Rawlings, she was told Ms. Graf would be with her shortly.

She heard a click. "Zoe?"

"Hi, Lara. How's everything going?"

"Fine. Just fine since you got me off the hook for those transactions."

"Yeah, well, that's the reason I called. Some new information has surfaced in the case."

Lara was slow to respond. "What information?"

"I have to talk to you, but not over the phone. I'm going to book a flight to Zurich for tomorrow."

"When you get the flight number, let me know and I will send a car."

Twenty-four

The western section of Istanbul is located in Europe; the eastern side is in Asia. Coop took the suspension bridge over the Bosphorus Strait and wove his way through the Asian section to an upscale neighborhood of condos and townhouses. The address given to Coop by Chief Fahri led him to an upstairs corner unit.

Coop knocked on the front door. Zoe stood next to him. An attractive woman, modestly dressed, opened the door. She wore a scarf over her face, which didn't hide her swollen and bloodshot eyes. Coop showed his credentials. "Excuse us, ma'am, we know this is a bad time, but..."

"What do you want?" she asked.

"We have a few questions."

"I'm tired of answering questions. Why can't you people leave me alone?"

"It's about your husband, ma'am."

"He's dead. Let him rest in peace."

Zoe nudged Coop aside. "Ma'am, we're so sorry for the intrusion. This ordeal must be very hard for you."

The widow stared at her shoes and tears began to roll down her cheeks. Zoe reached for her hand and gave it a tender squeeze. "We won't be long. I promise."

The woman opened the door all the way and led Coop and Zoe to the front room where packing boxes, some sealed, some partially packed, and some empty were scattered around the room. She motioned for Coop and Zoe to take a seat on the couch. "Will you take tea?" she asked.

"Thank you, that would be nice," Zoe said.

She excused herself and left for the kitchen. Coop and Zoe stood and began snooping. Coop started by picking through the boxes while Zoe browsed the room. She noticed several framed photos arranged on an end table; they were family pictures taken in happier times. She picked them up. One, a bit larger than the others, showed a handsome man standing proudly next to a six-foot bluefin tuna hanging from a trophy arch. A sign behind the man read: COCOS SPORTFISHING. Zoe held it up for Coop to see and then set the photo back on the table.

Coop felt a bit like a voyeur, picking through a family's personal items, but continued without remorse. He rummaged through the partially packed boxes: pillows, clothes, knick-knacks, and books. He began sorting through the books, but did a double-take when he spotted a paperback that looked familiar. It was the same one he had seen on Saraaf's desk; the one written in Arabic with the cover that showed an island surrounded by sparkling turquoise water. Coop heard the widow returning. He dropped the book back into the box and he and Zoe returned to the couch.

The widow set the tray on the coffee table and poured a cup of tea for each of them. Coop had no intention of drinking it, but he added a spoonful of sugar and stirred it around. Zoe liked tea and took a couple sips. She was the first to speak. "Our sympathy for your husband."

The widow spoke softly, "Thank you."

Zoe pointed to the large picture on the end table. "That's a nice photo. Is that your husband?"

She glanced at the picture. "Yes, he loved deep-sea fishing."

"It must be difficult seeing reports every day in the papers and on TV."

"I loathe those news people. They all blame my husband for what happened. I know it wasn't his fault. He was a good man. He was a good pilot. It wasn't his fault."

Coop continued to stir the tea. "I'm sure it wasn't."

The widow's face turned hard. "I curse the day that man talked him into leaving Air Iran."

"A man? What man?" Coop asked.

"An Indian man. He talked my husband into working for Burma Airlines."

"Who was this man?"

"I don't know. I tell everyone I don't know. He looked important with his nice suit and smooth talk. I don't know his name."

Coop stood and ambled toward the packing boxes. "Looks like you're moving."

"Yes, the children are already with my parents back in Iran. We will live with them."

He reached into a box, removed the familiar book and held it up for the widow to see. "Have you read this?"

She shook her head. "I don't read many books. I was going to throw it out, but it was among my husband's things, so I kept it."

Zoe could feel the woman's anguish. She caught Coop's eye and jerked her head toward the door. They stood and thanked the widow, returned to their car and headed back to the Bosphorus Bridge. "Have you ever gone deep-sea fishing?" Zoe asked.

"No. Why?"

"I'm just curious what Cocos Sportfishing is all about."

"I dunno, it doesn't interest me."

Coop's phone buzzed. Zoe lifted it from the console and checked the ID. She handed it to Coop. "It's Fran."

He flipped open the phone. "Fran? Is Josh okay?"

"He's fine, but Gordon's had an accident."

"An accident? What kind of accident?"

"A car hit him in a crosswalk."

"How bad?"

"Real bad, but he keeps mumbling that he needs to talk to you. Can you get back here?"

"I can try."

"Try hard," Fran said, and hung up.

Coop turned to Zoe. "Gotta go back to D.C. for a day or two." He felt a cough coming on and covered his mouth. A couple of drops of blood hit his hand.

"Where did that come from?" Zoe asked.

He looked at his hand and wiped it on a piece of Kleenex. "I had a bloody nose this morning. Must be leftover stuff. Listen, I want you and Marco to head back to Baghdad and wait for me there."

"I'll send Marco back right away, but I have to go to Zurich first."

"I thought you might."

Twenty-five

Zoe joined the parade of passengers disembarking the flight. She wore jeans, a sweatshirt, and sneakers; a far cry from the tight dress, boots, and fur worn on her last Zurich trip. After exiting the immigration area, she spotted a man in a blue suit holding up a sign that read: Ms. Kate Rawlings. Zoe raised a finger and caught his eye. He relieved her of her carry-on, but she hung on to her computer.

It was close to 9:30 p.m. by the time the black Mercedes pulled up in front of the Swiss Commerce Bank building. The driver escorted Zoe into the lobby where she signed in with the attendant as an after-hours customer. He pointed to the elevator. "Ms. Graf is expecting you."

Lara was waiting as the elevator doors opened on the top floor. She managed a weak smile. "I'm not sure what's more appropriate, a hug or a handshake."

Zoe put her arms around her. "A good hug never hurt anyone."

They went into Lara's private office and she headed for the bar. "Scotch okay?" Zoe nodded and Lara poured two generous portions into double old-fashioned glasses. They settled into a pair of soft leather chairs. "I've missed you," Lara said.

Zoe let a sip of Scotch tease her palate. "I've missed you too."

"Is this trip all business?" Lara asked.

"Maybe, maybe not. We'll see."

"Then let's get rid of the business."

"Okay. When you helped me get hold of Amacher's computer files, you told me you weren't involved in any of his Iraq transactions. You said you only suggested your clients as potential buyers."

"And that is the truth. You said on the phone that additional information has surfaced on the case. What is this information that has given you reason to doubt my word?"

Zoe took her computer from the case and set it on the coffee table. She inserted the flash drive and typed in the password. "I thought you might want to see an encrypted file we took off Amacher's computer." She rotated the laptop so Lara could view the screen.

Lara read through the financial details; her eyes widened and her brow furrowed. The sale was described as a purchase of Iraq collectibles from a seller John Doe #1, to a buyer John Doe #2, for the price of $10,000,000. The down payment of $1,000,000 cash was paid in advance on September 1st and the balance of $9,000,000 cash was to be paid in 30 days. The $2,000,000 broker commission would come out of the final payment. The last line of the file had the broker's electronic signature: *Lara Graf, Swiss Commerce Bank, Zurich, Switzerland.*

"This is absurd. I have never seen this document, let alone signed as its author."

"How does an electronic signature get on a document?" Zoe asked.

"Swiss Commerce has a master account with an e-signature transaction management firm. Every officer in the bank is registered and has a personal password to identify themselves before any signature can be authorized on a document."

"So, someone got your password and signed as you?"

Lara slammed the laptop cover shut. "Someone? It was that son of a bitch, Amacher. He's hiding behind my signature." Her hands were trembling.

Zoe went to the bar, refilled their glasses and handed one to Lara. She took a large slug and waited for the alcohol to seep into her bloodstream. Zoe didn't say a word.

Five minutes passed before Lara broke the silence. "After you confronted me with Amacher's dealings in the Middle East, I checked the bank's computer records. Almost all of his deals in Iraq must have been shadow deals."

Zoe leaned forward. "Shadow deals? What are shadow deals?"

"They're disguised transactions. Amacher uses the bank's name, but the deals never show up on the bank's records and the bank never gets a cut."

"It doesn't sound as if our banker is very ethical."

"Hardly. He'd be fired on the spot if the bank found out."

Zoe mulled it over for a few minutes. "I want you to confront him. Don't tell him how you found out, but tell him if he doesn't cut you in, you'll expose him."

Lara was taken aback. "But why?"

"Look, this isn't about art relics; it's something way bigger than that. We know the final payment is going to be made on the first of October, but we don't know where. Amacher must know because the seller is going to pick up the remaining nine million and Amacher's going to want his two million commission before the fortune disappears."

Lara processed the information, "Okay, I'll do the best I can."

Zoe loaded her computer into the case. "You have to let me know as soon as you have the location."

"Of course," Lara said. She sank into the soft leather and threw her head back. "You know what? This cloak and dagger stuff gives me an appetite."

"What did you have in mind?"

"I have two bottles of two-thousand and five Chateau Margaux-Margaux maturing in my cellar. I've been saving them for a special occasion. How about we kill them with a wedge of two-month-aged Fontina?"

Zoe glanced at her watch. "Sounds great, but it's almost ten-thirty and I haven't arranged a hotel yet."

Lara leaned over and touched Zoe's hand. "I don't think that will be necessary."

~ * ~

The next day Lara arranged for a limo to take Zoe to the airport while she headed straight to the bank. She walked right past Amacher's secretary. "He's expecting me." She opened the door to his private office and burst in without knocking.

Amacher was his usual obsequious self, fawning over Lara's outfit and her jewelry. When he ran out of compliments, he said, "So, Lara, you implied this meeting was urgent."

"Christophe, it's come to my attention that you've been running a big shadow deal in the Middle East."

"I don't know what you mean."

"Sure you do."

Tiny beads of sweat broke out on Amacher's forehead. "Lara, we all have a skeleton or two in our closet. You know that. My God, you and I have worked together on a couple of shadow deals."

"Those were borderline. The clients I sent you for those deals were all personal friends."

"Well, nonetheless, we worked outside the bank."

Lara laughed. "Those deals were for a few hundred thousand dollars. I'm talking about the ten-million-dollar deal you brokered in Iraq."

"How...?"

"How? How is not the issue. Do you deny you forged my electronic signature on that agreement?"

Lara's gaze was like a laser penetrating Amacher's brain; he opened his mouth, but no words came out. Eventually he mumbled, "yes...yes I did."

"Why?"

He stammered a few disjointed sentences, but wasn't able to provide a reasonable answer. Instead, he said, "What do you want, Lara?"

"I want the two-million dollars."

"What? The entire commission?"

"Unless you want the bank president and the board to hear about this."

"Okay, look, I'm willing to work this out, but not the whole commission. How can you justify that?"

"The same way you justified forging my name. You made me the fall guy just in case this deal was discovered. What you didn't factor in was the possibility that I would be the one to discover it. Well, I did and now it comes down to basic economics. I'm taking all the risk, so I'm taking all the reward."

Tears welled up in the corners of Amacher's eyes. "Lara, please, I'm heavily in debt. I need the money."

Lara stood and walked toward the door. Amacher pleaded. "Please, please..."

She turned. "I know the money is being delivered on October first. Where is it being delivered?"

"I...I don't know yet. I'm to be notified forty-eight hours before the transaction; the first is still a week away."

She handed Amacher a tissue. "When you're notified, you will inform them that I, not you, will collect the commission. Then you will let me know immediately."

He dabbed his eyes with the tissue. "Of course, but what about... what about...you know...something for me?"

"You don't deserve it, but because of our long friendship I'll give you five-hundred thousand."

"Oh, thank you, Lara." Amacher made an effort to hug her, but she backed away. "I understand," he said. "I'll let you know the delivery spot as soon as they notify me."

Twenty-six

Izmir Air Base, the closest U.S. facility to Istanbul, was two hundred miles away. Coop decided instead to pay for a commercial red-eye to D.C. and charge it out on his budget as a miscellaneous expense.

Coop exited the D.C. arrival gate along with two hundred other blurry-eyed passengers. He was making his way to the exit where the taxis lined up, when an elderly woman walking in the opposite direction stumbled and fell to one knee. Coop stopped to help her to her feet. As he turned, he made eye contact with a man behind him. The face looked familiar, but before he could identify it, the man darted into the men's room.

The woman got to her feet. "Thank you, young man."

"My pleasure, ma'am." Coop looked into the men's room. One guy was at the urinal; a couple of others were washing their hands. They didn't look familiar. He turned toward the stalls. Under one door he could see a pair of shoes partially covered by rumpled trousers. Coop looked at his watch. He had to get going.

There was a fifteen-minute wait for a cab, so Coop fell into line and dialed Dr. Goodman's number. After a receptionist, an assistant, and a PA, the doctor finally came on the phone. "Hello, Mr. Cooper, are you back?"

"Just for a few hours. I thought I'd check in. Any good news?"

There was a short pause. "I'm afraid not. The biopsy showed a squamous cell carcinoma."

"That's bad, right?"

"Let's just say it's not good."

"Shit, is there any treatment?"

"Definitely. We'll start with chemo followed by radiation...then there's always the option of surgery."

"What's the prognosis?"

"If we get on it right away, it's pretty good. If we wait...let's just say, it's not good at all."

Coop thought about Zoe and Marco waiting for him in Baghdad. "Doc, I have to put it off a couple of weeks."

"I recommend against it. The longer you wait, the greater the chance it will metastasize."

Coop reached the front of the taxi line. "I understand. I'll call you as soon as I'm back for good. Anything I should do for now?"

"Yes, stop smoking," he said. Coop thanked him and got into the front seat of the cab.

A hospital volunteer, an elderly woman with gray-blue hair, directed Coop to the Intensive Care Unit. When the elevator doors opened, he spotted Fran near the nurse's station. He gave her an awkward hug. "How is he?" he asked.

Fran didn't hug him back. "A little better. My sister is with him."

"Which room?"

"Five-o-two."

Gordon was lying face-up with his eyes closed. He had several tubes going in and a couple coming out. His wife Myra, Fran's sister, was holding his hand. Coop gave her a peck on the cheek and wanted to say something consoling, but nothing came out.

"He's been asking for you," Myra said. She excused herself and left the room.

Coop gently touched Gordon's shoulder. He opened his eyes. "Coo...Coop?"

"How ya doin', buddy?"

"I saw it, Coop...saw the security tape."

"Gordon, it can wait."

"No...it can't wait. Flight five-seven-one...five trucks...lion's head logos. Gordon closed his eyes for a moment. He opened them again. "They tried to kill me."

"Kill you? Who tried to kill you?"

"Somebody...somebody in the Agency."

"Gordon, that doesn't make sense."

"Every time I tried to open the security tape, someone... someone on my system blocked it. I had to do an end-run to get in."

"Are you sure?"

"Sure, I'm sure. I can tell when I'm being watched on a computer. Someone was there, I could feel it and..." Gordon closed his eyes again. Coop lifted the water glass and put the straw to Gordon's lips. He took a sip. "...and when I came out of the building, a car—a big black sedan—deliberately ran the light and hit me.

Coop patted Gordon's shoulder. "It's okay. Get some sleep, we'll talk later."

Gordon touched Coop's hand. "Coop?"

"Yeah, Gordon."

"Something awful is happening here, Coop." He squeezed Coop's hand. "Be careful."

Coop joined Fran in the hallway. She wasn't smiling. "You got Gordon mixed up in this junk of yours, didn't you?" she said.

He took a deep breath. "Well, sorta."

"Why would you do that? He's a nerd, not an agent."

"It was important."

"Important to you, maybe."

"I knew I could trust him."

"You mean use him. So you can find your mystery shooter."

"No, so I can find the gold."

"Really? Do you even care about the gold?" Coop didn't answer. "Never mind. Josh needs to know when you're coming back for good."

"Soon."

"I don't have any idea what that means. What do I tell him?"

"Tell him I'll talk to him before I leave," Coop said. Fran turned and went back into Gordon's room, leaving Coop alone in the hallway.

He called a taxi and waited outside the hospital entrance. He had the craving for a cigarette, but thought about Dr. Goodman's advice and was able to resist the urge. When he saw a cab turn the corner and approach the hospital, he waved, but before the taxi reached him a black sedan cut in front and screeched to a halt next to the curb. The passenger window slid down and Coop recognized the man he had seen in the airport. "Hey, McNamara," Coop said. "What's with all the special attention?"

"Hey, Coop. I don't really know, but the deputy director wants to see you...like right away."

Twenty-seven

McNamara and his partner, a twenty-year man named Tillson, escorted Coop into the deputy director's office. Randy was sitting behind his desk with his hands clasped and his thumbs tapping against each other. He motioned Coop to take the seat facing him.

Coop took out a pack of cigarettes. "Mind if I smoke?"

"Yeah, I do mind. You can wait."

He dropped the pack back into his pocket. "Okay, so why the escort?"

"Why didn't you tell me you found the gold?"

"Because I didn't find it."

"That's not what I heard."

"Well, you heard wrong."

Randy reached in a drawer and pulled out a three-week-old newspaper. The headline and the entire front page were devoted to the Burma Air passenger jet that went missing over the Indian Ocean. He threw it on the desk in front of Coop. "You tracked the gold to Flight five-seven-one."

"Is that what Marco told you?"

"Never mind who told me."

"Well, fuck Marco. That wimp doesn't know what the hell he's talking about."

"Write up your report. This mission's over."

"No, it isn't and you'll get a report when I've finished the operation."

Randy stood and pointed a finger at Coop. "I said it's finished."

"And I said it isn't."

"Hand over your badge."

"What? Why?"

"Because I'm tired of your bullshit. You're done at the Agency."

Coop threw his badge at the desk and it ricocheted onto the floor. "I'm gonna finish this mission—with or without a badge."

"You think so? Give me your passport."

Coop gave Randy the finger and started for the door. Randy motioned to Tillson and the agent grabbed Coop by the shoulders and pushed him against Randy's desk. Coop struggled and Tillson landed a punch over his right eye. Coop broke loose and fired back with a fist that bent Tillson's nose, spattering blood across the open newspaper. McNamara rushed to Tillson's defense and the two men managed to restrain Coop.

Randy's eyes were angry. "Take his passport."

McNamara looked up at Randy. "What the hell are we doing here?" he said. "The guy's just trying to do his job."

Randy glared at him. "Shut up and get that passport."

Coop began to struggle again and Tillson pushed his head down against the desktop. Coop was face to face with the cover of a book. It was the same one he had seen in Saraaf's office and the same one that was in the pilot's house.

McNamara reached into Coop's breast pocket and extracted his passport. He handed it to Randy. "Now, get him out of here." The two agents pushed Coop toward the door. "McNamara," Randy said. "You stay here."

Tillson forced Coop out of the office and McNamara approached Randy's desk. "Sir?"

"Who am I?" Randy asked.

"Sir?"

"Who the fuck am I?"

"You're the deputy director."

"And I'm your boss. Who the hell do you think you are questioning me?"

"I apologize. I just thought..."

Randy pointed his finger. "You're a dumb Mick. You're not paid to think." McNamara swallowed hard. "I don't know why they even let you people in the Agency. You're all drunks and retards."

McNamara's face was flushed and he began to perspire. "Sir, I..."

"Do you intend to ever move up in this Agency?"

McNamara wiped his forehead. "I do, sir."

"Well, you're not going anywhere under my watch. You understand?"

"Yes, sir."

Randy glared at him and gave a dismissive gesture. "Now get the hell out and don't fuck up again or you'll end up just like Cooper—out of the Agency."

Twenty-eight

The alarm flashed 5:15 a.m. Coop reached across the pillow, turned off his phone and staggered out of bed to the bathroom. The 5 x 5 room was lit by two fluorescent bulbs, but only one was working. He didn't expect much more for thirty-eight bucks a night.

He looked in the mirror. He hadn't shaved in three days; his hair was a mess and his right eye was still swollen half shut. He managed to get a trickle out of the shower and washed yesterday off his body.

Darkness was giving way to a faint stream of morning light when Coop walked to his car and brushed a thin layer of frost from his Chevy's windshield. He glanced up the street. A black four-door sedan with exhaust vaporizing from its tailpipe was parked near the corner.

Coop turned onto the boulevard leading downtown and looked in his rear-view mirror. The sedan was a few car lengths behind. He glanced again at the mirror when he turned into his office building garage; the sedan was pulling into a parking spot across the street.

At this time of the morning, all the offices were empty. Coop passed several rows of cubicles before stepping into his office. He inserted his ID card into the computer and waited for the screen to light up: USER CANCELLED. "Shit." He pulled out his card and tossed it into the wastebasket.

He took the elevator to the basement and slipped out through the back door. The weather matched his mood. The temperature had dropped a couple degrees, reached the dew point and a heavy fog was forming. He walked around the block, crossed the street and came up behind the black sedan. Cigarette smoke was drifting through the driver's half-open window. Coop took out his Glock, shoved it through the opening, and pressed the muzzle against the driver's temple. "Goddammit, McNamara. why are you on my tail?"

McNamara kept staring straight ahead. "Randy's orders."

"He fired me. Why does he even give a shit where I go?"

"I don't know, I just do what I'm told."

"Yeah, what if he told you to shoot me? Would you do it?"

McNamara cautiously turned his head. "Coop, what the hell's going on?"

"Better you don't know. Clasp your hands together and touch the roof."

McNamara did as he was told. Coop snapped a set of cuffs on McNamara's wrists and opened the door. "Move over," he said. McNamara slid across to the passenger side and Coop got behind the wheel.

"Where are we goin'?" McNamara asked.

"Never mind. Give me your ID card."

"My what?"

"Your ID card. Where is it?"

"I...I don't have it with me."

"Don't give me that bullshit. Where is it?"

"Come on, Coop, I can't.

"Goddammit, McNamara, I'm not fucking around here." Coop reached into McNamara's inside coat pocket and slipped out his wallet. He rummaged through the cards: a Mastercard, a Blue Cross card and a podiatrist appointment reminder. "Where is it?"

"You know I...I can't. Randy's just looking for a reason to boot me out."

Coop moved the pistol in front of McNamara's left earlobe. "Mac, I don't want to do this. Don't make me. Just give me the ID. I need it."

"Coop, plea..."

Coop pulled the trigger. The tip of McNamara's earlobe disappeared, along with most of the passenger side window. He reached for his ear and blood dripped onto his shackled hands. "Oh shit, what the fu..."

"The card, where is it?" Coop said.

McNamara shook his head like he was trying to get water out of his ear. "I can't hear. I can't hear you."

He turned McNamara's head and spoke into his other ear. "Where's the card?"

"Seat, under the seat. Christ, you blew my eardrum out."

Coop reached under the seat and moved his hand around until he found the card. "Password."

"I can't...I can't hear."

He pushed the pistol against McNamara's right ear. "July, with a capital J," McNamara said.

Coop put his pistol back in the holster, started the car and headed for the on-ramp to I-95 heading north toward Baltimore. About ten miles past Bethesda, he turned off the freeway and headed west into a rural area of Maryland. A sign for County Road 37 appeared and Coop made the turn. The road was paved for a while, but turned into dirt about five miles in. Ice was beginning to form on the frozen mud as Coop inched along the road that led to an eventual dead end. He parked the car, opened the trunk and took out a tire iron. "Get out," he said.

McNamara looked ominously at the tool and did as he was told. The bleeding had stopped, but his ear was a mess. Coop pointed up ahead to an old hunting shack and McNamara trudged toward it. Coop used the tire iron to pry off a couple of two-by-fours that were nailed across the door and then nudged McNamara inside.

The shack was almost bare except for a potbelly stove, a stack of wood, a canvas cot and a six-pack of water. Coop unholstered his pistol. "Wrists," he said. McNamara raised his hands; Coop unlocked the cuffs and backed away. "Take off your pants and shoes."

"Come on, Coop."

He liked McNamara and knew him to be a good guy, but this was a binary choice—either McNamara was with him or he was against him. "Just take 'em off...please," Coop said.

McNamara kicked off his shoes, loosened his belt and dropped his trousers. "Now what?"

"Roll 'em in a ball and slide 'em over to me."

McNamara did as he was told. He began to shiver and held his arms around his chest. "Look, I don't want to get you canned. If this password works, I'll make sure I take the fall for you," Coop said.

"Put fourth on the end. You get it? Julyfourth with a capital J."

"Yeah, I get it, thanks. Listen, it's supposed to get warmer in a day or two. The nearest phone is about five miles down the road." Coop slid his cigarette lighter across the floor. "This'll get the stove going." He picked up the bundle of clothes and walked out. He hesitated, went back inside, and set McNamara's shoes on the floor. "Sorry, man. Maybe someday we can be friends again."

Coop drove back to D.C. and headed straight to Josh's school, where he parked near the curb and kept his eye on the vacant schoolyard. At two o'clock sharp, the recess buzzer sounded and kids swarmed onto the playground. He spotted his son and approached the fence. "Josh, hey Josh," he yelled.

Josh jogged to the fence. "Hi, Dad. Mom said you were back."

"Hi, buddy. You look great."

"You look awful. What happened to your eye?"

Coop touched his eyebrow. "Oh, this? I walked into the bathroom door."

"Mom said you don't live with us anymore."

"Listen, Josh, don't worry about it, everything will be all right. I'll be back for good real soon."

"She cries a lot."

Coop looked away and bit his lip. "I know it's hard on you and Mom, but I have something I just have to finish."

"But I don't want you to leave."

"I know you don't. Hey, how's Rusty?"

"He's okay, but he cut his paw. Mom let him sleep on my bed." The buzzer sounded again and the kids headed back for the doors. "I have to go," Josh said.

Coop pushed two fingers through the fence. "Gimme a squeeze."

Josh squeezed Coop's fingers. "Dad."

"Yeah, Josh."

"Don't let anyone kill you."

Twenty-nine

Coop drove around for an hour before he spotted a Cinemark 12. He spent the next six hours jumping between theatres and then killed some more time grabbing a bite at the hamburger joint next door. By the time he finished his third cup of coffee, a large wall clock chimed eleven. He dropped a twenty on the table and left.

The Agency annex garage was only a mile away. Coop parked McNamara's car next to his Chevy and took the stairs to the second floor. He passed the cubicles, slipped into his private office and sat down in the dark at his computer. He inserted McNamara's ID card and typed July4th. The screen lit up.

He typed RANDY NICHOLS on the keyboard and waited. A 25-year-old photo of the deputy director appeared on the screen. He scrolled through Randy's bio until he reached the year 2006, then he clicked on it and a new window came up.

Station Chief: Baghdad, Iraq
American Ambassador: James Billings
Co-agent: Craig Cooper

He scrolled to 2005.

Station Chief: Baghdad, Iraq
American Ambassador: James Billings
Co-agent: Craig Cooper

Coop thought he heard the door open in the outer office. He quickly scrolled to year 2004, but before the window appeared, the office door opened and a security guard holding a weapon walked in. "Get away from the computer and identify yourself," the guard said.

"Ralph, it's me, Craig Cooper."

"Sir, you're no longer allowed in this building."

Coop feigned surprise. "What d'ya mean? Since when?"

"Since five o'clock this morning, sir."

"It's some kind of screw-up. I'll get it straightened out."

"Step back, sir."

"Hey, this is sensitive information, I can't just leave it on the screen."

The guard waved his pistol. "You need to exit this office right now or I'll have to arrest you."

Coop raised his hands. "Okay, okay, I'm leaving." He backed away from the computer, but took a glancing look at the 2004 window that was still displayed on the screen.

Station Chief: Baghdad, Iraq
American Ambassador: James Billings
Co-agent: Marco Torelli

Coop rode the elevator to the lower level and pushed the door open to the near-empty garage. He stopped at Mac's car, placed the ID, the ball of clothes and the ignition key on the driver's seat, then fired up his Chevy and left through the Independence Avenue exit. He drove through the remnants of the old tenderloin district and about a mile beyond spotted what he was looking for—a used car lot with a blinking sign that read: OPEN 24 HOURS. Coop checked the Chevy's clock; it was a little after midnight.

Half-a-dozen floodlights illuminated the lot. Coop drove in and parked next to a tiny kiosk that apparently housed the executive offices. The door opened and a guy dressed in a parka and a loosely fitting tie shuffled out to greet him. "Ya lookin' for something new?" he asked.

"Not really," Coop said. He patted the hood of his Chevy. "What'll you give me for this baby?"

The salesman circled the car, scrutinizing every scratch. He rubbed his hand across the paint and looked inside to feel the leather seats. "Needs a little work," he said.

Coop coughed and his breath turned into fog as it hit the freezing air. "Cut the bullshit. It blue books for eighteen-five."

The salesman ignored the reference and popped the hood. "Engine looks pretty good. How many miles?"

"Forty-eight thousand."

"You got the pink slip with you?"

Coop patted in his breast pocket. "Yeah, right here."

"Okay, I'll give you top dollar—ten-five."

"No way. Fifteen-five."

The salesman laughed. "I'm thinking twelve."

"I'll take fifteen even."

"Thirteen-five. Final offer."

"How 'bout fourteen?"

"Thirteen seven-fifty...cash."

"Come on, you can do better than that."

"Okay, I'll pay for your cab."

Coop handed him the pink slip.

The taxi pulled up in front of Union Station. Coop passed the car salesman's twenty to the driver and told him to keep the change. The driver gave him a blank stare. Coop glanced at the meter as it clicked to $19.25. He laughed and dug out an extra five and handed it to the guy.

The train station was quiet with the homeless stretched out on benches as they settled in for the night. The only noise came from the janitor's mop as it sloshed back and forth on the tile floor. Coop tapped on the ticket window. The clerk's head popped up and he looked at Coop with bloodshot eyes. "Can I help you?" he asked.

"Anything to New York tonight?"

The clerk ran his finger down a schedule. "There's an Amtrak at four twenty-two."

"That'll work." Coop peeled a twenty from his wad.

Thirty

Most of the shop owners had already folded back their iron gates and were open for business by the time Coop emerged from Penn Station. He didn't bother with a cab; the walk would do him good.

He spotted a sign in the window of a diner: BREAKFAST $5.99. He went in and chose a booth in the corner. A waitress with dyed hair, gray roots and too much eye makeup came to his table carrying a glass of water and a couple utensils wrapped in a paper napkin.

Coop ordered two eggs, toast and coffee. When the waitress took his order back to the kitchen, he removed his cell from his pocket and tapped a number in his phonebook. It only took two rings before the call was answered. "Hey Boss, how goes it?"

"Hey, Zoe, things aren't going well. In fact, the sky's falling."

"That bad, huh. How's your brother-in-law?"

"I'll tell you about him later. Are you in Baghdad?"

"Yeah, I got back this morning."

"Good, I'm getting on the first flight I can find. I want you to pack lightly and get away from the embassy ASAP. I'll call you when I get in."

"Uh, oh. This doesn't sound good. Okay, I'll wait for your call."

"And Zoe, just so you know. Marco's out of the loop."

He mopped the yolks with a piece of dry toast and finished his coffee. Then he opened his cell and copied all the numbers from his phonebook onto a paper napkin before leaving ten bucks on the table and heading for the restroom. There was only one stall. He removed the lid from the reservoir tank, dropped his phone into the water, replaced the lid and left the diner.

He checked the time and stepped up his stride. It was getting late. Times Square with its sleazy shops and sordid lifestyles was only eight blocks away. He broke into a jog until he spotted what he was looking for—a beat-up unmarked door sandwiched between a massage studio and a tattoo parlor. He banged on it as he looked up at the security camera. A voice came through the speaker. "Coop, is that you?"

"Hello, Victor."

A buzzer sounded, the door popped ajar and Coop stepped inside. An octogenarian with a goatee, long gray hair and a ponytail greeted him with a smothering hug. He gave Coop a long look. "That's some eye you're sporting. I'm guessing you're still in the spy business."

"Yeah, I'm too dumb to do anything else."

Victor laughed and pointed to a staircase. "Come into my office. We'll catch up."

Coop did a quick study of the room. It was no bigger than two hundred square feet, but it housed a glut of equipment and supplies. The centerpiece was an HP desktop computer hard wired to a high-tech printer. Stacks of blank passports, driver's licenses, and birth certificates were piled against the wall and in the corner a tripod held a 35mm camera that faced a stool and a white screen background.

Victor opened a desk drawer and pulled out a bottle of Wild Turkey. "Too early to celebrate a reunion?"

Coop looked at his watch. "Nine-fifteen? Perfect."

Victor poured healthy portions into a pair of paper cups and handed one to Coop. He raised his cup. "To old friends." Victor tapped Coop's cup and they both drained the Kentucky bourbon in one gulp. "So, what brings you to my palace after five years?" Victor asked.

"I need a driver's license and a passport. How much for an old friend?"

"U.S. or somewhere else?"

"U.S."

"I owe you a favor. How 'bout four grand?"

Coop grimaced. "I'm really tight on cash. How's two thousand and we call it square?"

Victor opened a drawer and took out a jar of pancake makeup. He used two fingers to spread it over the bruise under Coop's eye and pointed to the stool. Coop took a seat and Victor snapped a half dozen full-face photos.

An hour later, Victor performed his magic and handed Coop a U.S. passport and a New York State driver's license. "Here you are Mr. Hayes—Mr. Christopher Hayes."

He examined the documents. As usual, the old man's work was perfect. "Thanks, Victor, you're the best." He stuffed them in his pocket and took out a beat-up phone. It was the one he had taken from the morgue after going through Ted's belongings. "Hey, buddy, how about one more favor," Coop said.

"Billable or non-billable?" Victor asked.

"I'm afraid I need this one on the house." He handed Victor Ted's phone. "Can you get this thing working long enough to find out what's on it."

Victor turned the cell over a couple times. "How long was it in the water?"

"A day maybe."

He pulled out a set of tools that looked as if they were designed for a watchmaker. Using a small screwdriver, he carefully popped the back off the phone and with miniature tweezers he withdrew the memory card. He slipped it into a slot on the front of a computer and turned on the screen. Several numbered codes appeared, and Victor tapped on one that brought up a list of phone numbers. He pointed to the screen. "Here's the last number this phone called."

Coop peered at the screen. It was his number. "There should be some photos. Can you get to the them?"

Victor chose another of the numbered codes. A couple of dozen photos appeared.

"Which are the most recent?" Coop asked.

Victor pointed to the bottom row. "These four."

"They're blurred."

Victor tried to adjust the clarity, but the pictures were still unreadable. "Sorry, it looks like whoever took these didn't hold the phone steady enough."

"Could you print out all four of them anyway?"

He handed the photo prints to Coop and gave him another crushing hug. "Be safe, my friend."

Coop headed back to the train station where three Airporter shuttles were lined up and loading passengers. He paid thirty-one bucks and took a seat on the first van in the fleet.

JFK, as usual, was swarming with people. Coop checked the international departure screen. Only two flights were leaving for Baghdad: United at eleven forty-eight and Qatar at one-twelve. Common sense told him to stay away from any American carrier; he stepped to the Qatar counter. Victor's work passed the test and Coop purchased an economy seat on the flight to Baghdad with a stop at Hamad International in Doha.

Coop hopped off the Terminal 4 walkway and spotted a shop selling souvenirs. He bought an *I Love New York* sweatshirt, a Yankees baseball cap, a Statue of Liberty backpack, and a pair of dark sunglasses. He found the nearest men's room.

The security lines leading to the international departure gates were a mess. Coop was in no hurry and fell into line behind an older couple who reminded him of his nana and papa. When he was in range of the X-ray conveyor belt, he spotted two guys off to the side wearing blue blazers and dark sunglasses and definitely overacting their nonchalance. Coop tugged his visor down over his glasses. One of the guys said something to the other and they both headed straight for the line in which Coop was waiting.

He sized up the situation. An escape route didn't exist, so he bent over to tie his shoe as the agents came storming in his direction. They rushed past him and approached a man several spots ahead. The guy handed the agents his passport and while people strained their necks to see what was happening, Coop slithered out of line and walked to the rear.

He watched and waited. He'd been in this business long enough to know that the reward for a little patience was usually a big opportunity. Fifteen minutes later, a woman juggling an infant, a diaper bag and a carry-on joined the line.

Coop slipped in next to her. "Need help?" he asked.

The woman looked around to see if Coop was talking to her or someone else. "Excuse me?" she said.

"You've got your hands full. I can carry the diaper bag and the suitcase for you."

"Oh, I couldn't."

He reached for the bags. "It's no problem. Really."

The woman touched his arm. "You're a doll. Thank you."

They approached the conveyor belt where the agents were eyeballing the checkpoint. The woman bent over to remove her shoes and the baby started to cry. Coop set down the cases and said, "I'll hold her for a minute." He took the baby in his arms and glanced at the agents. They were looking right past him.

Thirty-one

Coop joined the throng of comatose passengers making their way to the Baghdad baggage claim. Everything he had with him was in his backpack, so he broke from the crowd and stepped into a shop selling an assortment of electronic devices. A salesman, who recognized Coop as an American, was on him immediately. "Looking for a computer, perhaps?"

"No, do you have any burners?" The salesman looked bewildered. "You know, pre-paid, throw away phones," Coop said.

The salesman smiled and pointed. "Yes, yes, follow me." He led Coop to a case filled with a wide assortment of cell phones, slid the glass door open and took out a bare-bones model. "This one is best. Ten hours for thirty-thousand dinars."

"What's that in dollars?" Coop asked.

The man took a calculator from his pocket and tapped a couple of buttons. "Twenty-five and sixteen cents."

Coop dropped three twenties on the counter. "I'll take a couple."

Coop rented the cheapest car he could find—a five-year-old stick shift. Before he took off for the city center, he activated a phone and punched in a number, one of the many he had copied onto the napkin before he trashed his old Motorola. Zoe answered, "Who is this?"

"It's me," Coop said.

"Oh, hey boss, how goes it?"

"I'll tell you later. Are you familiar with the Hotel Fatima?"

"That dump downtown?"

"That's the one. I'll be checked in under the name Christopher Hayes. See ya there."

~ * ~

Coop was lathered up and in the middle of a shave when he heard a knock on the hotel door. He opened it for Zoe, who took one look at him and broke out laughing. "What?" Coop said.

"A white foam face with a black eye. You look like you belong in the circus."

"Well, if this gig doesn't work out, maybe that's where my next job will be. Come on in."

Zoe looked around the room: a double bed, a lamp, a two-drawer dresser, and a mirror. "Guess you went for the deluxe, huh?"

"We're short of cash; Randy's not footing the bill anymore. Make yourself comfortable while I finish up."

Zoe reached into her backpack and pulled out a Glock. "I dug up an extra. Thought you might need it."

Coop took the pistol, rolled it over in his hand and smiled. "That's why I love you. Hey, are you hungry?"

"Yeah, it's almost midnight. I didn't have dinner."

There was a coffee house next door to the hotel that served small plates all night. Coop and Zoe ordered the first two on the menu and chose a table away from the cigar smokers. "So, what happened to the eye?" she asked.

"One of Randy's goons."

"What? Why?"

"Marco jumped the chain of command."

A waitress approached and set down a couple of plates of pastry shells filled with some sort of meat along with two mugs of coffee. Zoe waited for her to leave. "So, Marco talked to Randy. So what?"

Coop dug into the food. "Randy ordered me to close down the operation. I wouldn't do it."

"So he had you beaten up?"

"And took my passport. I'm traveling on a Victor Special."

"I don't get it. What am I missing?"

"Are you ready for this? Marco worked in Baghdad with Randy the year before I got here."

Zoe dropped her fork on the plate. "You've got to be kidding. Marco?"

"And Billings acted like he'd never met him. Let's get another cup of coffee. We're going to be up late tonight."

~ * ~

Zoe was the only one with credentials to get into the Green Zone, so she did the driving. The guard at the West Gate looked over Zoe's documents and Coop's passport, then peered in at Coop. "My brother," Zoe said. "He just got in from the States." The guard nodded and waved the car through. She drove past Coop's old apartment house and parked across the street from the embassy building. She turned to Coop. "What am I looking for?"

Coop handed Zoe the printouts of the photos Victor had recovered. "These are off Ted's phone, but they're unreadable. The originals are somewhere in Billings' office. I want them."

Zoe looked across the street. "Getting into the building will be easy. I don't know about Billings' office."

Coop pulled a set of keys from his pocket and dangled them between his thumb and forefinger. "Ted's," he said.

Zoe took the keys, hustled across the street and strolled through the double doors leading to the entry hall. A guard sitting at an elevated desk looked down from his perch. "Ma'am?"

Zoe passed her papers and her badge to the guard. While he copied Zoe's information onto a log, she asked, "Are you new here, Corporal?"

The soldier, who looked like he wasn't old enough to buy beer, handed back her credentials. "Yes, ma'am. It's my second week."

Zoe smiled. "Hey, you can drop the ma'am stuff." She extended her hand. "I'm Zoe Fields."

The guard knew the place was empty, but he looked around just to make sure. "I'm Charlie, Charlie Santos."

They shook hands, but when Charlie attempted to withdraw his, Zoe hung on. "Are you married or have a girlfriend back home, Charlie?"

The young man blushed. "Not really."

"Maybe we could get together sometime."

"Sure, I guess. Whenever you'd like."

Zoe let go of his hand. "Look, Charlie, I'm in a bind. I lost this document that frankly I don't think is very important, but unfortunately my boss does. I'm in deep doo-doo if I don't find it. How long do I have upstairs?"

Charlie looked around again. "It's supposed to be a half-an-hour, but you can stay as long as you want."

Zoe winked. "Thanks, I'll see you on my way out." She stepped into the elevator and pushed the button for the top floor.

One of the big keys got her into the outer office and a smaller one allowed her entry to Billings' private space. Ted spent a lot of time looking through the bookshelves, but Zoe was a pro; she went straight for Billings' desk.

There was nothing of interest on top; she started through the drawers. In the middle drawer, next to the condoms, was an 8 x 10 photo. She matched the profile from one of Victor's fuzzy prints to the picture. She slipped it under her shirt.

Zoe took a small case of picks from her pocket and used one to open the lock on the bottom drawer. She removed a stack of letters and documents from the drawer and after inspecting each one, she carefully replaced them. Under the pile was a folder labeled: FRIENDS. She dumped the contents on the desktop and a dozen full-face photos spilled out. One by one she held the faces of the clear photos next to Victor's blurry print. The sixth one in the stack was a match.

She concealed it under her shirt with the other photo and placed the rest back in the folder. She locked the desk drawer and turned off the lights.

Coop looked at his watch; Zoe had been gone for over an hour. He went back to eyeballing the embassy doors. One of them opened and Zoe, accompanied by a corporal, stepped out. Coop watched as Zoe smiled and handed the young man a piece of paper. She headed for the car and the corporal went back inside.

Zoe slid into the driver's seat and looked at Coop, who was smirking. "What?" she asked.

"I thought the guy's zipper would pop. I'm guessing you gave him your number."

Zoe smiled. "Actually, I gave him Marco's and told him to call me when he gets off at 4 a.m." They both broke up laughing.

"Any luck up there?" Coop asked.

Zoe handed him the 8 x 10. It was a picture of a beautiful Middle Eastern woman striking a sexy pose. He turned it over. The inscription on the back read: *To my beloved Jim. I look forward to our Thursday afternoons together. Hasana.* Coop smiled. "Looks like our strait-laced ambassador has a dark side."

Zoe smiled, "You think?"

"Let's see the other one." She passed it to him. He squinted. "Ghazali."

She nodded. "Turn it over."

Coop flipped to the back side. It read: *A.N. (Karbala).* "What the hell do those initials stand for?"

"Beats me. A nickname, maybe?"

"For Sahir Ghazali? I doubt it."

Thirty-two

Coop, dressed only in boxers, rolled out of bed and tiptoed into the bathroom. When he returned, Zoe, was awake and was sitting on the end of the bed wearing one of Coop's long T-shirts. "Just like old times," Coop said. "Only without the sex."

"It was like old times. You took up the whole bed and snored all night."

He laughed. "Get dressed, we'll grab breakfast and then I'll show you where the shootings took place."

The alley was dirtier, and the buildings were shabbier but other than that, the place hadn't changed much since the night Coop was shot and Mustafa was killed. Coop parked in the general area where Ahmad had parked and he and Zoe got out of the car. He surveyed the alley and the buildings that lined it. A chill ran down his spine. He motioned Zoe to follow as he paced off about twenty yards. He pointed to the ground. "As well as I remember, this is where Mustafa went down. I got hit between here and the car."

Zoe checked out the scene and pointed to a 2nd floor window in the adjacent building. "Did the shots come from there?"

"That's what Ahmad said."

"So, you were a sitting duck. I'm surprised he waited 'til you were almost at the car."

Coop looked back and forth between the car and the spot where he was standing. "I don't know, but Ahmad said the shot sounded different."

"How so?"

"He couldn't put his finger on it."

"Where do we go from here?" Zoe asked.

"It's Thursday. I'm going to find out if Billings still has the same girlfriend. I'll drop you at a cab stand; see what you can dig up on the ballistics."

The West Gate of the Green Zone was the closest to the embassy building. Coop parked thirty yards away where he had an unobstructed view of vehicles going in and coming out. The hours ticked by, but Coop stayed focused. He was rewarded when, just after two-thirty, a black Mercedes with diplomatic plates pulled up behind the gate and was waved through to exit the Green Zone. Coop fell in behind and followed as the car wove through a suburb of Baghdad.

The Mercedes pulled up in front of an apartment house; Coop parked next to the curb ten yards back. The driver jumped from the car, opened the back door and Billings stepped out. He pointed to his watch and said something to the driver before he disappeared through the entrance to the apartment house.

The Mercedes took off. Coop sprinted to the building and entered the lobby just in time to see the elevator dial stop at floor number five. He pushed the button and waited for the elevator to return.

The fifth floor had only five apartment doors. Coop put his ear to number 501, but there was no sound inside. He moved to 502 and cupped his ear against the door. He heard a man and woman talking in a flirtatious tone and the man sounded like Billings. Coop took out his Glock, rammed his shoulder against the door and when it sprung open, he burst in. A gray-haired woman who was watching a soap opera on TV turned toward him and shrieked. Her eyes looked like they would pop from their sockets.

Coop lowered his pistol and backtracked to the door. "Sorry... sorry...mistake." He took a few bills from his pocket and set them on a table as he backed out the door and closed it behind him.

He made his way down the hall. No sounds were coming from inside number 503 or 504. He put his ear to the last one in the hall— 505. A man and woman were giggling. With his pistol still in his hand, he kicked the door open and bulled his way in. Billings and the beautiful woman from the photo were on the bed, half-naked and locked in an embrace. The woman pulled the sheet over her breasts and an angry Billings sat up. "Cooper, what the fuck?"

Coop's smile was humorless. "Hello, Mr. Ambassador. How's your afternoon goin'?"

Billings' eyes turned to slits. "You fool, every MP in Baghdad is looking for you. What do you want?"

"We have to talk."

"I have nothing to talk to you about. Get your sorry ass out of here."

Two bathrobes were draped over the foot of the bed. Coop tossed them to Billings. "Cover yourself up and get rid of your girlfriend."

He put on a robe and the woman, who by then was sobbing, ran into the bathroom still clutching the sheet. "You're a prick, you know that? I have no idea why Randy ever hired you," Billings said.

"You mean to replace Marco?"

Billings face paled. "Look, Randy told me Marco was working on a covert operation and you didn't need to know about it."

"You're a shitty liar. You lied about not knowing Marco and you lied about not knowing Ghazali."

"What are you talking about?"

Coop reached into his pocket and took out the photo of Ghazali. He flipped it to Billings. "This came out of your bottom drawer."

He stared at it. "How the hell did you get into my office?"

"I'm a spy...remember?"

"So, what do you want from me?"

"That's a picture of Sahir Ghazali, the guy you said you didn't know."

"Yeah, I know this guy, but his name's not Ghazali."

"Bullshit."

Billings handed the photo back to Coop. "His name is Nasir...Ali Nasir. Check for yourself, his initials are on the back."

He didn't need to check; he knew they were there. "Why was his picture in your drawer?"

"He's one of our snitches. He worked both sides. What you guys call an asset."

Coop was having trouble wrapping his head around what Billings was saying. "Randy gave me a file that had his name as Ghazali. Now you say his name is Nasir."

"So what?"

"What d'ya mean, so what?"

"These guys have a million aliases. What do you care? Find him and find out for yourself."

"I did find him. He had a bullet through his forehead."

"Well, that's how most snitches end up. Case closed."

The bathroom door opened and the woman came out, but before Billings could offer any soothing words, she grabbed her clothes. "Hasana, there's nothing to be afraid of. Please..." Hasana scurried back inside the bathroom and slammed the door.

"If you didn't know Ghazali, why did you give Marco that phony address?" Coop asked.

"So, that's what this is all about? Look, I'm telling you for the last time, I never had a file for a guy named Ghazali and Marco never showed up at my office and I never gave him any address. Now get the hell out of here."

Thirty-three

Zoe gave the taxi driver a U.S. ten, told him to keep the change and entered the hospital through the emergency room entrance. It looked a lot less intimidating than it had when she had come through on a gurney. The same intake nurse who checked Zoe in that night was on duty. "May I help you?" she said.

"Do you recognize me, by any chance?"

The nurse did a double take. "Oh, for sure. You're the one that was rolled in here with a bullet hole in your arm."

"You have a good memory."

"It looks like your arm is working pretty well. What brings you back?"

Zoe took out her badge and her credentials and set them on the desk. "I'm actually a U.S. government agent. I need to see the records for a couple of gunshot victims that were treated here about a year ago. One died."

The nurse looked at the credentials. "Not a very good picture of you."

"Yeah, I know. I had a hangover."

The nursed laughed and handed the papers and shield back to Zoe. "The record room you're looking for is on the second floor."

Zoe took the stairs and approached the only door on the floor. She entered and was taken aback. An older man in a white lab coat looked up from the cadaver upon which he was performing surgery. His surprised expression showed in spite of the mask he wore over his nose and mouth.

"Oh, I'm sorry," Zoe said. "I thought this was the records room."

The man removed his gloves and took off the mask. He kind of looked like Albert Einstein without the mustache. "Who are you?"

She showed her badge. "Government agent—intelligence."

"My, oh my, there're making spooks a lot prettier than they used to."

"I guess that's a compliment," Zoe said.

"It is. What can I do for you?"

"I need to talk to someone about some records. The nurse sent me here, but..."

"What kind of records?"

"Gunshot victims."

"That would be me."

Zoe looked confused. "I don't understand. I assume you're a pathologist or something like that."

The man laughed. "I am. Call me Doc. All the gunshot cadavers come through here and I keep the records." He motioned toward a couple of chairs. "Come, we'll talk. It's not every day a pretty girl visits me." He unfolded a TV table and set it between the chairs. "How about some coffee? Maybe a donut?"

She really didn't feel like eating with a corpse in the room, but it was what it was. "Sure, black's fine," she said.

Doc poured two coffees and took a donut from a paper bag. He cut it in half and set it on a paper napkin next to the coffee cups. "My last one. You mind sharing?"

"Not at all."

The old man leaned forward and dunked the pastry into his coffee. "Old habit," he said as he stuffed the soggy dough into his mouth. "Which of my patients are you interested in?"

Zoe took a sip of coffee. She was pretty sure it was made with yesterday's grounds. "An Iraqi guy named Omar Mustafa. He was probably brought in here last year on the thirty-first of December."

Doc pointed to the half of untouched pastry. Zoe waved her hand. "Actually, I'm cutting down on sugar. Be my guest."

He scooped up the remainder of the doughnut and wolfed it down as he searched a file drawer. He found what he was looking for and dropped a folder in front of Zoe. "I have to finish up with the gentleman over there. Take your time."

Zoe pushed the coffee aside and started through the folder. It was written in medical jargon, most of which she didn't understand, but one phrase got her attention. *The bullet passed through the left carotid artery and lodged in the trachea one centimeter below the larynx.* She inched toward the dissection table. "Doc, where's the bullet?"

He looked up from the gore. "Bullet, what bullet?"

"The one you took out of Mustafa's trachea."

"It's in a drawer with a thousand others."

Her heart sunk. "Please tell me it's marked and that you can you identify it."

"Of course, my dear, I'm extremely organized, but..."

"But what?"

"I can't give it to you. It's like inventory. It has to be accounted for."

Zoe squinted. "Doc, how many times this year has anyone come looking for a bullet?"

Doc interrupted his procedure again, took off his gloves and shuffled to a large cabinet where he pulled out a small Tupperware bowl. He handed it to Zoe. "I guess you're the first," he said.

She plucked the bullet from the bowl, dropped it into her pocket and planted a big kiss on his cheek. "Thanks, Doc, you're the best."

Zoe took the stairs back to the emergency room. The same nurse was on duty and Zoe approached her again. "Hey, thanks for the directions. I was wondering, though, where would I find the records for the victim that didn't die?"

"Oh, yeah, I forgot one guy made it. Most of them don't. Fifth floor, but watch out...she's a bitch."

"Thanks," Zoe said. She handed the nurse a twenty-dollar bill. "Could you buy the doc on the second floor a couple of pounds of fresh coffee?" The nurse laughed and took the twenty.

Zoe entered through a door with a placard overhead that read: SURGICAL RECORDS. She showed her credentials to the clerk who said, "I'm very busy today. What do you want?"

"I need to see a record for last New Year's Eve—December thirty-first."

"Why?"

"I...I really can't tell you."

"Well, I really can't help you."

"Please, I need it."

"That's your problem. Bring an order from your station chief."

A tear ran down Zoe's cheek. "This isn't business. It's personal."

The clerk handed Zoe a Kleenex. "What do you mean, personal?"

She dabbed her eyes. "I'm sorry, my husband was shot the night before. He was operated on here, but he died on the plane back to the States. I was hoping the file could bring me some closure."

The clerk took a deep breath and exhaled through her nostrils. "What's the name?"

"Craig Cooper."

The clerk opened a file cabinet, rolled out a drawer and removed an accordion folder. She handed it to Zoe. "There's a lounge next door."

"Thank you," Zoe whispered.

She opened the folder. The report said the bullet went straight through Coop's back and lodged in his right lung. Three surgeons took four and a half hours to get the bullet out, along with a lobe from his lung. He was in critical condition and airlifted to Landstuhl Military Hospital in Germany. Ten days later he was flown back to D.C.

Zoe tried to slip the records back into the folder, but something kept them from going all the way down. She looked inside. A plastic baggie was stuck in the bottom. She reached in, pulled it out and turned it upside down. A bullet fell out.

Thirty-four

Coop got back to the hotel before Zoe and peeked into the lounge. It was no bigger than his room, but it housed a short bar, five stools and one table for four. Coop ordered a beer and exchanged small talk with the bartender. It was an interesting conversation as the bartender spoke very little English and Coop spoke even less Arabic.

"Any book stores around here?" Coop asked.

"Buk? What is a buk?" the bartender said.

"Not buk...book." Coop placed his outstretched hands together as if reading from his palms.

The bartender tossed his head up and down. "Yes, yes...buk."

Coop had to chuckle. "Okay," he said. "Any buk stores around here?"

The bartender pointed to the east. "One hundred meters."

Coop thanked him and left a five-dollar bill. East was to the right, so Coop headed in that direction and wove his way around street vendors, keeping an eye on the storefronts. Their names were all written in Arabic, but one caught his eye. It had a rack of newspapers out front and there were people inside who Coop could see were reading. He went in.

In addition to newspapers written in several languages, the store had shelves covering every wall; they were all stocked with books. Coop approached the proprietor and began describing the cover of the book he was looking for. Unfortunately, the language barrier got in the way and Coop knew it wasn't going to work. He thanked the man as best he could and went directly to the shelves.

It was an arduous task—removing and replacing books. After several hours, he came upon a small area that contained a section of books that appeared to be geographical. Many had a map, or an outline of a country, or a continent on their covers. He gave the shelves a cursory look. Then he felt a chill run up his back. The spine of a thin paperback had a familiar turquoise color. He pulled it out. The turquoise was indeed water and in the middle of the cover was an island.

This was the book Coop had seen three times before: Saraaf's office, the pilot's home and Randy's desk. But he had never been able to look inside. He took a seat in the corner and leafed through the pages. Unlike the colorful cover, the pictures inside were black and white. Some were of the ocean, some of various islands and several were maps and graphs. They all had captions written in Arabic. Coop bought the book and headed back to the hotel.

Coop was positive Zoe wouldn't be found hanging around their room, so he looked into the lounge. She was plopped on one of the five barstools where a guy twice her age was hitting on her in a foreign tongue. Coop strolled up and planted a juicy kiss on her lips. "Hi honey. Let's grab that table," he said, pointing to the only one in the bar.

They sat and Zoe took a sip from her beer. "Thanks. I was getting ready to deck him."

"He never would have seen it coming. So, any luck today?"

Zoe reached into her pocket and took out the two bullets. She dropped them on the Formica where they sounded like a couple of dice hitting a craps table. Coop picked them up. "Where did you get 'em?"

"From the hospital—one from surgical, the other from the morgue."

"These can't be right."

"They are, though. The big one came out of Mustafa and the small one came out of you."

"The guy had two guns?"

"Or there were two shooters."

Coop looked at his phone. It was only four o'clock. "Let's take a ride."

There was a parking spot across the street from the Smoke Shop and Coop grabbed it. They dodged the traffic and went inside. The big guy rose to his feet and blocked access to Sami. "Relax," Coop said. "I come in peace."

Tiny looked at Sami, who waved him off. "Mr. Coop, come in. We are still friends. Yes?"

"Yeah, we're still friends."

Sami looked through his inventory. He removed two cartons from the shelf and handed one to Coop. "For my long-time friend." He looked at Zoe and raised his brows.

"No thanks, I'm allergic to tar and nicotine."

Coop accepted the offering and looked inside. "Thanks. Hey, are you still in the favor business?"

Sami's gold tooth glistened. "Of course."

Coop reached into his pocket and took out the two bullets. He dropped them on the counter. "I need one. Do you know someone who can identify what type of weapons fired these?"

Sami picked them up and studied them. "Perhaps."

"You do or you don't?"

"I do, but he is very expensive."

"How expensive?"

"Two thousand."

Coop took out his bankroll of hundred-dollar bills, peeled off twenty-five and handed them to Sami. "Twenty for him and five for you."

Sami reached for the bills. "Very generous, Mr. Coop."

"But I need the information by tomorrow," Coop said.

"Give me your number. I call you."

Thirty-five

Zoe woke first but decided to stay put and let Coop get some much-needed sleep. A half-hour later he opened his eyes and saw her staring at him. "You checking out my gray hairs or what?"

"No, I was just thinking how long it's been since I woke up two mornings in a row with the same person."

"Yeah? That only proves sex gets in the way of good relationships."

"So, you're saying if we had sex you'd have been gone in the morning?"

He laughed. "No, I was thinking you probably would."

Coop's phone rang while he was in the shower. Zoe answered and walked into the bathroom where Coop was lathering his hair and didn't hear her come in. She poked him in the ribs; he almost hit the ceiling. Zoe handed him the phone. "Sorry," she said. "I think it's your cigar buddy." She was right. Sami gave Coop an address and told him to be there at eleven o'clock.

He wasn't familiar with that section of the city, so he hailed a cab and handed the address to the driver. He was expecting a sleazy office in a scuzzy part of town, but when the taxi pulled to the curb, they found themselves in the most upscale section of Baghdad. All the properties were large and all were fenced and gated. Zoe and Coop approached a brass box equipped with a microphone-speaker. Coop pushed the arrival button.

A voice speaking in Arabic came through the box. Coop leaned in. "We're Sami's friends." A buzzer sounded and the gate swung open, revealing a long circular drive that led to a stately looking mansion.

As they approached the house, a man dressed in an ankle-length robe opened the door to greet them. "Mr. Farzad is expecting you," he said. Coop and Zoe followed him into the house. Coop knew these homes still existed, but he'd never been in one. It was opulent: high ceilings, marble floors, gold leaf and ornate furniture.

Their guide led them to a large parlor. "Please make yourselves comfortable. Mr. Farzad will join you shortly." He bowed and left. Coop and Zoe settled into red velour armchairs and looked around the room. It was perfectly appointed. The only out of place item was a security camera mounted in a corner of the ceiling.

The double doors opened and a tall, handsome man, dressed in suit and tie strode into the room and thrust out his hand. "Kasim Farzad."

Coop extended his. "Craig Cooper." He gestured toward Zoe. "My partner, Zoe Fields."

Farzad kissed the top of Zoe's hand. "My pleasure. May I offer either of you a drink?"

"Whatever you're having," Coop said.

He opened an antique cabinet and removed three snifters along with a decanter filled with an amber-colored liquor. He splashed a generous portion into the glasses and handed one to Zoe and another to Coop. "This is now forbidden in my country, but I have a source." He raised his glass and tapped it to theirs. They let a sip of the powerful alcohol slide down the back of their throats.

Farzad reached into his pocket and withdrew the two bullets. "So, Mr. Cooper, our mutual friend gave me these to examine. May I ask where they came from?"

Coop took another gulp of liquor. "One from a dead guy's neck and one from my lung."

"I see." He dropped the large bullet on the table. "I assume this one is from the deceased. It most likely came from a Tabuk Sniper Rifle."

"Never heard of that one."

"It's the weapon of choice for Iraqi marksmen. There are many men in graves because of this weapon." He set the smaller bullet next to the other. "And this one...I can't be sure, but I think it came from an American made pistol."

"Really? Any idea which one?"

"Again, I can't be positive, but the markings suggest a Glock. Most likely a twenty-two or twenty-three."

"That's interesting. Thank you, Mr. Farzad."

"My pleasure. Is there anything else I can help with? It's included."

Coop thought for a minute. "Yeah, I heard that Saddam hid a fortune in gold before he was captured. Do you know anything about it?"

"I have heard that rumor, but I doubt its veracity."

"Really? Why?"

"I knew Saddam. He was clever. If he had a large amount of gold, he would have turned it into cash. That would be easier to hide."

"So you think it's a fable?"

"If I had to bet on it? Yes."

Coop thought for another moment before taking the torn half-photo of Ghazali from his pocket. He handed it to Farzad. "I was wondering, do you recognize this man?"

Farzad examined the torn photo. "Yes, this man was one of Saddam's bodyguards."

"Do you remember what name he went by?"

"I do not, sorry. But if you look closely at the rifle he is holding, you will see it is one of the Tabuk Sniper Rifles I described to you."

Coop took back the photo and was able to make out the telescopic lens. Farzad showed just a hint of a smile. "And, if you have another thousand dollars in your pocket, I will supply you with something you will be quite interested in seeing."

Coop frowned. "I thought you said additional info was included."

"Yes, I did. But this is special, this will cost you."

Coop dug deep and dropped ten one-hundred-dollar bills on the table. Farzad went to his desk, opened a drawer and removed a photo from a folder. Coop immediately recognized it as an undamaged copy of his torn photo. Ghazali was smiling and holding the rifle. Another man was doing his best to look away, trying to hide his identity from the camera. He didn't succeed; his physique and profile were unmistakable. It was Marco.

"May I ask how you got a hold of this? Coop said.

"Certainly. After Saddam was executed, a black marketeer sold me several photos from Saddam's collection. I knew someday they would be valuable. Today is one of those days."

"Thank you, Mr. Farzad. You've been a great help." Coop dropped the bullets and the photos into his pocket.

Thirty-six

Coop and Zoe weren't used to heavy alcohol before lunch, especially when they hadn't eaten breakfast. Now, they needed food. The coffee house next to the Fatima was convenient.

The place wasn't packed, but Zoe recognized some of the same men who had been there when she and Coop shared a midnight snack a few nights ago. The regulars were congregated in the back and by pushing several tables together they were able drink, smoke and jaw. Only four tables were available—all in the front of the restaurant. Coop and Zoe took one.

An old man, probably the owner, approached their table. "American?" he asked. They both raised index fingers. "Welcome, welcome. Something to drink? Something maybe to eat?"

Zoe looked at the menu. Unfortunately, it was written in Arabic. "What is that wonderful smell?" she asked.

"Kubba...very good."

"Kubba? What is kubba?" Zoe asked.

The man pointed to a picture on the wall. "Kubba."

Zoe still wasn't sure what it was, but the sweet aroma won her over. She ordered one for each of them along with two coffees. She grinned at Coop. "So, did I screw up?"

"No, it's as good as it smells. It's lamb with this stuff called bulgur; some kind of a couscous made from wheat or something like that."

The kubba was delicious and the thick brown coffee neutralized the alcohol attacking their stomach lining. They scarfed up in silence. When their plates were empty, they stopped to take a breath and Zoe belched. "Whoops, where did that come from? Sorry."

Coop smiled. The smile turned to a laugh and the laugh turned into a cough. A couple drops of blood hit his hand. "Are you okay?" Zoe asked.

He waved her off. "Fine, I'm fine. Hey, what went through your mind when Farzad said he didn't think Saddam would hide gold?"

"It made sense, but he doesn't know what we know—the warehouse, the five trucks, the missing airliner..."

"Yeah, that's exactly what I was thinking too."

The door opened and a scruffy guy in his twenties wearing a baseball cap and carrying a backpack, shuffled in. He took a seat at the table next to Coop and Zoe, and set his pack underneath it. He ordered a coffee and lit a cigarette.

Zoe waved her hand in front of her nose. "Deodorant alert."

"You wanna move?" Coop asked.

"No, let's just get going."

He called for the check. The guy next to them snuffed out his cigarette, gulped down his coffee and headed for the door. Coop's head drew back like a deer sensing a predator. He scanned the room and then looked at the vacated table next to them. His eyes narrowed as he caught sight of something underneath it. The guy's backpack was still there and a faint red glow was filtering through the nylon fabric.

Coop grabbed Zoe by the arm and dragged her out the door. Before she could ask what was going on, a blast from inside blew the door and the windows from the building. Coop and Zoe were knocked to the ground as flames and flying debris came belching through the openings.

"Are you okay?" Coop asked.

"Yeah, we better get outta here."

Sirens screamed as Coop and Zoe made their way to the hotel next door.

Zoe didn't bother to fold her clothes; she just shoved them into her carry-on. Coop, who only had a backpack, was already packed and ready to go. The lobby was chaotic; people were screaming and moaning and paramedics were giving aid to the injured. Coop put his room key and a hundred-dollar bill on the counter. He and Zoe made their way to the exit.

"Who knew I was back?" Coop said.

She gave it some thought. "Well, Billings for sure...your cigar buddy Sami and his friend Farzad..."

"...and Randy must have figured it out," Coop said.

"...and he probably told Marco," Zoe added.

Coop checked the date on his watch. "Today's the twenty-seventh. The payment for the gold is going to take place in four days. When is Lara supposed to let you know where?"

"She said as soon as Amacher gets the word, she'll pass it on to me."

"We can't wait." He waved his hand at a taxi and they hopped in. Coop took out the wrinkled napkin containing his old, scribbled phone numbers. He tapped one into his burner phone. "Hey, it's Coop, can we come over? We need to talk to you."

The driver knew his way around the city and got them there in less than ten minutes. Ahmad opened the apartment door and motioned toward the living room. "Come in, come in."

"Sorry to barge in on you like this," Coop said.

"It's not a problem. Please, sit." Ahmad looked them over. Their clothes were torn, their faces were scratched and their hands were filthy. "I don't wish to be rude, but you both look as though you came through a war. What happened?"

"A bomber tried to take us out," Zoe said.

Ahmad's brow lifted. "The coffee house? I saw it on TV."

"Yeah, did they say how many people were killed?" Coop asked.

"Just one. Apparently, he was the owner."

Coop shook his head. "Shit. The poor guy was just trying to eke out a living."

Ahmad's wife entered with a pot of coffee and a plate of sweets. She poured three cups and left the room without speaking. They sipped their drinks. "Does this mean you may be getting close to the gold?" Ahmad asked.

"Maybe." Coop handed Ahmad the book he had bought the day before. "Take a look at this. What the hell is it about?"

Ahmad looked at the cover and leafed through its contents, only reading a page here and there. Coop and Zoe silently drank their coffee and munched on the cookies, giving Ahmad as much time as needed. When the cookie plate was empty, Ahmad closed the book and placed it on the table. "It's a kind of a geography-slash-geology book."

Coop furrowed his brow. "A what?"

"It's titled, *Missing*. It's the chronicle of an island in the Indian Ocean." Zoe set her cup on the table. Ahmad continued, "The island disappeared in the late fifteen-hundreds."

"What d'ya mean disappeared?" Coop said.

Ahmad lifted the book from the table and handed it to Coop. "Take a look at the old maps. The island was on a trade route charted by a Portuguese spice trader back in 1508. Sixty years later, a big earthquake shook the Indian Ocean and the island must have crumbled into the sea. The traders never saw it again."

Coop flipped through several pages of maps, then pointed to one on the last page. "That doesn't make sense. If it disappeared, why is it on this map?"

Ahmad leaned over to see which map Coop was referring to. "Take a look at the date on the bottom."

Coop looked below the picture. "1998? What...?"

Ahmad pointed to the Arabic narrative next to the picture. "This says, 'in 1998 an Australian trawler, looking for new waters to fish, discovered this unnamed island jutting out of the ocean approximately two and a half feet above the surface. It is believed to be the same island that disappeared in 1568.'"

Zoe scratched her head, "How's that possible?"

"Coral growth," Ahmad said. "It's actually pretty interesting. It says here that geologists figure it must have started growing on top of the original island's rock crumble and four centuries later it reappeared. It's in the middle of nowhere, so no one noticed it until that fishing boat happened on it a few years ago."

"It just looks like a dot on this map." Coop said.

"That's what it is. A speck in the middle of the ocean. Look at the scale. It can't be more than a mile wide and three miles long."

Zoe leaned in to take a look and she pointed to the top of the map. "What are these larger islands up here?"

Ahmad rolled his finger along the paper. "Those? Those are the Cocos. They look to be about three-hundred miles north."

Coop's head snapped to attention. "The Cocos Islands."

"Sound familiar?" Zoe said.

"Yeah, sport fishing, maybe?"

Thirty-seven

The taxi let them out on the street and Coop and Zoe walked the remaining twenty feet to the gate. Coop pushed the button on the cement column and a familiar Arabic-speaking voice came through the speaker. Coop spotted a surveillance camera and looked straight at it. "It's Craig Cooper and Zoe Fields. We met with Mr. Farzad earlier today. Our apologies, but we have to speak with him again." There was a two-minute pause before a buzzer sounded and the gate opened.

They were led to the same room where they had met earlier with Farzad, but this time they didn't have to wait; he was seated behind his desk. "Back so soon?" he asked.

"Our apologies, Mr. Farzad, but an urgent matter has caused us to intrude," Coop said.

"No intrusion at all. Please sit down. A drink, perhaps?"

They settled into a couple chairs facing the desk. "Thanks, but no drinks. I'll get right to the point of our visit. There's been an attempt on our lives and we need to get out of the country and to a major airport. Is this something you could arrange?"

Farzad clasped his hands and twiddled his thumbs. "The coffee house bombing, I presume. If I may ask, where is your final destination?"

Coop hesitated. He was putting their lives in Farzad's hands. "The Cocos Islands," he said.

Farzad stroked his chin several times while processing the information. "Obviously, you can't leave from Iraq, so that leaves Turkey or Syria. Turkey would be my first choice, but the Istanbul airport is heavily surveilled. I would, therefore, suggest Syria—Damascus International." He paused before delivering the closing line. "I hate to broach the subject, but this is an expensive endeavor."

Coop knew it would come down to money, something he had little of. "How expensive?" he asked.

"Ten thousand dollars."

His brain churned through a quick calculation of his finances. "We can give you four thousand now and a promissory note for six."

"A promissory note? Do you mean an I.O.U.?"

"It's a matter of mutual trust, Mr. Farzad. We must trust you won't give us up and you must trust we will make good on our promise to pay."

Farzad gave it a few moments of thought. "Very well. Do you have the down payment with you?"

Coop reached into his pocket and removed his bankroll—a rapidly diminishing wad. He peeled off forty, one-hundred-dollar bills and placed them on the desk. Farzad gently scooped up the bills and stood. "I'll have some food brought in while I make arrangements. Plan to leave at dusk."

Coop thanked Mr. Farzad and said, "We have something important to take care of before we leave. Any chance you could loan us a car for a couple hours?"

"You do push the envelope, do you not, Mr. Cooper?"

"If it's a problem..."

This time Farzad laughed. "No, this is not a problem."

Coop knew Farzad had too much class to loan them a Toyota or Ford, but even Coop was impressed when the chauffeur parked a Mercedes S550 in the circular driveway. "You would need me to drive?" the chauffeur asked.

"No, we're good," Coop said. "But, could I borrow your jacket and hat?"

The jacket was a size too large, but Coop knew no one would notice. The chauffeur's hat along with his own aviator sun glasses covered his face nicely. He took the driver's seat and Zoe got into the back. She draped herself with an afghan that had been left on the seat.

For some reason, the East Gate seemed to have the fewest guards. Coop pulled up next to the kiosk housing two sentries and a soldier with sergeant stripes who approached the Mercedes. "What is your business in the Green Zone?" he asked.

Coop turned toward the back seat. "Madame is here to see Ambassador Billings." The sergeant peered inside the car. Zoe looked down and pulled the covering over the lower part of her face.

"Who may I tell him is here?"

Zoe leaned forward and quietly said, "Tell him Hasana. He will know."

The soldier returned to the kiosk and dialed a number. He nodded several times before hanging up the phone. He approached the Mercedes with a visitor permit and handed it to Coop. "Take a hard right turn at the first intersection. The ambassador will be waiting." Coop thanked him and drove off.

Zoe threw the afghan on the floor and Coop tossed the chauffeur's hat and jacket on the seat next to him. "How long do we have?" Zoe asked.

"Five, maybe ten minutes tops before Billings figures it out."

Coop parked in front of his old apartment house. They jumped out and sprinted to the elevator. "What room is Marco in?" Zoe said.

"Third floor. Right next to the elevator."

"Are we taking him with us?"

"We have to. There's not enough time to get anything out of him here."

When the number '3' lit on the elevator panel, Coop and Zoe took out their Glocks. The doors opened and they rushed into the hall. Coop ran full force toward the apartment door and just before impact lowered his shoulder. The door shuddered and snapped open.

Coop led the way and Zoe followed. Marco wasn't there. In fact, nothing was there. The bed was stripped, the bath towels were gone and the closet was empty. "Let's get the hell out of here," Coop said.

He fired up the eight-cylinder Mercedes and peeled rubber as he headed for the gate. The guard saw the car approaching and sprung from the kiosk holding up his hands. Coop floored the gas pedal and flashed right by him.

When Coop was sure no one was following, he slowed down and worked his way through traffic. "Where do think Marco went?" Zoe asked.

"I have an idea, but ask me again in a couple of days."

Thirty-eight

Farzad's assistant provided them with garments to wear over their Western clothes. Coop put on a long robe with a traditional turbanlike headdress; Zoe covered herself with a head-to-toe dark burqa. Their driver, an overweight gentleman with a holster strapped across his sagging belly, tossed their bags into the rear of a new Land Rover. Coop looked the car over; it was loaded: supercharged, four-wheel drive, heavy-duty tires, and after-market roof lights.

Before they departed, Kasim Farzad appeared along with another assistant, who placed several boxes of food and drinks in the back of the Land Rover. Farzad shook each of their hands. "It's a twelve-hour trip. *Risalat wadae*," he said. "Farewell and safe journey."

In less than thirty minutes, the lights of Baghdad disappeared and other than the Land Rover's high beams, it was pitch dark. Coop took out his phone and speed dialed a number. It was answered in Arabic.

"Ahmad? It's Coop."

"Hey Coop, how're you doing?"

"We're fine. Headed out of the country. I just had to call and thank you...for everything."

"There is nothing to thank me for, but I'm glad to hear your voice again."

"You saved my life. I'm forever indebted."

"Well, in a way you saved mine, too. Until you asked me to go on that trip to Tikrit, I was without a job and wallowing in self-pity. Yesterday, I went back to the embassy and they rehired me. Tomorrow will be a good day."

"That's great, Ahmad." Coop was silent for a few seconds. "Listen, buddy, I don't know if we'll ever see each other again, but have a good life. You deserve it."

Ahmad choked out a reply. "You too, my friend. You too."

Coop and Zoe fell asleep, but two hours into the trip the car stopped and they both snapped to attention. Their driver turned around. "Pretend sleep," he said.

A vehicle with flashing lights pulled up behind them. Two Iraqi soldiers approached the driver and a lot of Arabic conversation took place. A soldier shined his flashlight into the back seat. Coop's turban was pulled over his forehead and Zoe's burqa showed only her closed eyes. More Arabic was exchanged between the driver and the soldier. The discussion ended when the driver handed over several dinars which the soldier stuffed into his pocket before waving them on.

Seven hours later, the driver pulled into a village and parked in front of a small dwelling. He knocked on the door and gave a few coins to a bearded man before returning to the vehicle. "We have permission to use the toilet," he said.

The house was nothing more than one large room with a bathroom attached. Four big brown eyes peeked over the blankets of a single bed as the husband and wife stood near their children.

After using the facilities, the trio piled back into the Land Rover and the driver handed out falafel sandwiches and bottled water. He fired up the engine and re-entered the dark roadway.

Coop looked at his watch. It was 2:18; they'd been on the road for almost nine and a half hours. The driver slowed and came to a stop at the side of the blacktop. "A problem?" Coop asked.

"The border—five kilometers ahead. We cannot cross with your American passports."

"How then?" Coop asked.

"We will cross through a mountain pass. Buckle your belts."

They pulled the straps as tight as they would go. Their driver turned on the halogen roof lights along with the high-beams and put the Rover's gearshift into LOW#2. He left the paved road and plowed through the sand toward a dip at the top of the hilly range.

Even with their belts cinched, Coop and Zoe's heads kept clobbering the ceiling, but the driver was relentless and the SUV kept climbing as rocks and gravel spewed to the side. When the nose of the Land Rover finally negotiated the peak and headed downhill, Coop and Zoe were able to make out the lights of a village. The driver bounced the vehicle back on to the road. "We are in Syria," he said.

The driver dropped them in front of Damascus airport and handed them their bags. Coop shook his hand and passed him a hundred-dollar bill. The man passed it back. "Not necessary. Good luck." He waved and drove off.

They entered the airport and went directly to the restrooms. When they emerged, their Middle Eastern garments had been discarded and their appearance matched their passport photos. They had some research to do. Coop took the airlines on the right and Zoe took the ones on the left; twenty minutes later they huddled in the lobby. "I didn't find any, how about you?" Coop asked.

"I got one. Guess who?"

"Surprise me."

"Burma Airlines. They have one trip a day to the Cocos. It leaves in about three hours, but it's pricey."

"How pricey?"

"Fourteen hundred each."

"Shit, I'm about out of cash."

Zoe waved her credit card. "I charged it."

Coop kissed her on the cheek. "I love you," he said.

The distance between Damascus and the Cocos is 4400 nautical miles, which translated into a flight of 10 hours and 22 minutes. On descent, at five thousand feet, the Airbus made a turn to line up for the final approach. Coop poked Zoe. She opened one eye. "Wh... what?"

He pointed out the window at a string of over twenty islands.

"Uh, huh," Zoe mumbled. She closed her eyes and didn't open them again until the tires squeaked onto the runway.

Coop grabbed his backpack and Zoe's carry-on from the overhead bin and they joined the exit line.

Although the Cocos are in the middle of the Indian Ocean, a couple of thousand miles from Sydney, they belonged to Australia and most of the people working on the islands were transplants from the mainland. The airport on West Island, the one on which Coop and Zoe had landed, was only a five-minute walk to the village where two hundred permanent residents lived. Most of them, in one way or another, depended on the tourist trade for their income.

High season was still two months away and the hotels, all five of them, were almost empty. The nearest one to the airport was an open air, one-story structure nestled between a dozen palm trees. It wasn't air-conditioned, but large paddle fans moved the humid air around the room and within five minutes of checking-in, Coop and Zoe were under mosquito nets sound asleep.

Thirty-nine

Zoe woke first and checked out the time. It was 9:20 p.m. and with only a sliver of the moon peeking through the clouds, the room was pitch dark. She tapped Coop's shoulder. He woke with a start. "What?"

"It's getting late. We better get going."

They showered and dressed in whatever fresh clothes they could dig from their meager supply. They both pulled on shorts and T-shirts; Zoe wore flip-flops and Coop slipped into a pair of running shoes he wore without socks.

They sought out the drinking establishment nearest the water—a dive creatively named The Waterfront. Its featured attractions were an antique oak bar, a three-piece band and a great assortment of Australian beers. This time of the year most of the patrons were locals.

Coop pulled out a stool for Zoe and they cozied up to the bar. The barkeep, a bleached blonde in a tank-top and cut-offs, set a couple of used coasters in front of them. "G'day folks. What'll it be?"

"A couple of beers," Coop said.

"Just tapped some Carlton Draught. That be okay?"

"Yeah, great." He took out a pack of cigarettes, gave it a look and put it back in his pocket.

The bartender returned with two overflowing mugs. "Ya here to fish or dive?"

Zoe used her index finger to swipe off the foam. "Dive. So who runs the best charter around here?"

The bartender pointed to the end of the bar. A fit, sun-tanned guy in his late thirties downed a shot with a single gulp and chased it with a full glass of beer. "We better get to him before he's plastered," Zoe said.

The bartender laughed and ambled to the end of the bar. She said something to the guy and pointed toward Coop and Zoe. The man picked up his mug, slid off his stool and took a seat next to Zoe. "Name's Liam. Margie says you're looking to do some diving."

Zoe thrust out her hand. "We sure are. I'm Zoe...this is my diving buddy, Coop."

Liam took Coop's hand. "Nice to meet ya. We don't get many Yanks out here, especially at this time of the year. Why so far from home?"

"We heard a German sub was sunk out here during the war. Thought it might be fun to explore it," Coop said.

Liam looked a bit baffled. "Really? I've been diving the Cocos for fifteen years...never heard of it."

Coop finished off his beer. "It's pretty far out. What's your range?"

"Whatever you want it to be."

"How 'bout six hundred miles round trip."

"Six hundred? You're kidding, right?"

"No, we're serious. Can you do it?" Zoe asked.

"Sure, I can do it—with extra fuel—but..."

Coop pointed to the end of the bar. "What kinda whiskey were you drinking, Liam?"

"Jameson...Black Barrel."

He looked for the bartender. She was near the end of the bar, resting her elbows on the oak surface and puffing on a Marlboro. Coop waved two fingers and raised his voice over the crowd noise. "Hey, Margie, can we get three Jamesons over here?" Margie waved back.

Liam rewound the conversation. "Are you sure about that sub?"

"Yeah, we're sure. Do you have a GPS on board?" Coop said.

"Yeah, but..."

Coop moved his face close to Liam's. "Look, Liam, we know where we want to go. Do you want to take us there or not?"

"Yeah, I want to take ya."

Margie set three overflowing shot glasses on the bar. Coop held one up. "Then to a successful trip."

Zoe tapped her glass to Coop's. "A successful trip." Liam raised his glass without adding any words and the three of them chugged the shots.

While Coop and Liam continued working out details, Zoe glanced around the room. The bar was rapidly filling with what appeared to be a hundred percent locals. A musical trio featuring a guitarist in a cowboy hat began playing country music and a dozen people dressed in shorts and tank tops crowded the center of the room to dance. The front door swung open and Zoe did a double take. She got a glimpse of an attractive blonde woman, obviously a tourist, stepping into the bar. The woman disappeared through the ladies' room door.

Zoe excused herself and headed toward the restroom. She peeked inside. The blonde was in front of the mirror touching up her lipstick. "What are you doing here?" Zoe asked.

Lara caught Zoe's reflection in the mirror and her expression took on the look of a kid caught with a hand in the cookie jar. "Zoe, I can't believe this. What a surprise."

Zoe didn't return the greeting. "I'm asking you again, what are you doing here?" Before Lara could answer, two young girls tumbled through the door, drunk and laughing. One of them wobbled inside a stall and began to puke in the toilet. "Let's get out of here," Lara said.

They stepped back into the bar. The room was filled with another dozen drinkers and the noise level was approaching the threshold of a rock concert. Lara raised her voice, but Zoe couldn't hear it. She handed Zoe a key marked 303. "I'm at the Windsurfer," she yelled. "Meet me there later tonight and I'll explain everything." She slipped out the door.

Forty-five minutes later, Coop and Zoe went back to their room and turned in for the night. Zoe waited to hear Coop snoring before she eased out of bed and used the light from her cell phone to throw on a pair of shorts and a T-shirt. She slipped quietly from the room.

Zoe passed the The Waterfront and looked at her watch. It was 2:35 a.m. The noise coming from the bar was even louder than two hours earlier. Half a block ahead she could see the Windsurfer's neon sign blinking on and off.

She inserted the key and slipped into room 303. Lara had recently gotten out of the shower and was dressed in a robe with her damp hair pulled back in a ponytail. She smelled of soap, shampoo and body lotion.

"Drink?" Lara asked.

"No thanks, I've had enough already."

Lara sat on the couch and patted a nearby pillow. Zoe sat next to her. "Okay," Zoe said. "Let's hear it."

"I'm here to pick up the two-million-dollar commission."

Zoe rose from the couch. "You what? You were supposed to call me as soon as you knew the location."

"Relax, Zoe. Please, sit... please. I have been trying for two days to get ahold of you, but you didn't answer. I had no choice; I had to come for the money."

Zoe thought for a moment. She hadn't had cell service since they left Baghdad. She sat back down next to Lara. "Sorry," she said. "What were your instructions?"

"I was told to check into the Windsurfer and someone would deliver the cash within three days. I planned to call you when I got back to Zurich." She placed her hand on Zoe's shoulder. "Please believe me."

"I believe you. Sorry for my knee-jerk, but our operation is starting to heat up and I'm a little on edge."

"So, that is why you're here?"

"Yes. I can't tell you much, but suffice it to say we think the goods are nearby."

Lara began to laugh. "Nearby? There is no nearby around here."

"Yeah, well, we'll see."

"Zoe, when all this is over, do you think we could talk about some sort of...you know...future together?"

Zoe went to the mini-bar and popped the top off a Becks. "I'd like to think so, but this won't be over for a while and..."

"You sound worried. Are you in some sort of danger?"

"I'm not worried. It's just, in my business, you never know what tomorrow will bring. Listen, Lara, you have to promise me if your contact shows, you'll take the cash and get the hell out of here; and if he doesn't, you'll still get the hell out of here."

Lara approached Zoe. "Okay, whatever you say. I promise." She took Zoe's hand in hers. "Is there any chance you can stay here tonight?"

Lara's fragrances filled Zoe's nostrils, but she fought them off. "I have to get back before Coop realizes I'm gone." She gave Lara a peck on the cheek. "I'll call you when I get back to the States."

Forty

Coop did some simple math. Liam's boat would likely do about thirty miles an hour. The island was three hundred miles south—so a ten-hour trip. An arrival during the daylight hours or early evening was out of the question; Coop told Zoe to sleep in and they'd head down to the boat sometime around noon.

The marina was home to a boat rental, a repair shop, a charter fishing company, a dive shop, and a supply store. Jutting into the water was a pier with twenty boat slips. Coop and Zoe stopped at the store. They bought a duffel along with two pairs of quick-drying water shoes, two flashlights, two waterproof fanny packs and a bottle of Jack Daniels. They emptied their stuff from Coop's backpack and Zoe's carry-on into the duffel along with the newly purchased items. They set off for the pier.

At the foot of the pier was an arch used to hang the catch-of-the-day trophy and a sign that read COCOS SPORTFISHING. Coop and Zoe stopped in their tracks. "That looks familiar," Zoe said.

Coop studied the sign. "Yeah, all we need is a pilot and a bluefin tuna." Coop looked down the pier where Liam was waving at them. He waved back and they headed for the end of the dock.

Liam was standing in front of a sleek 41-footer with front and rear decks, a flybridge and cabin that housed a galley, four berths, and a head. Four fuel barrels were lashed to the decks next to a four-man dinghy. Liam noticed his passengers weren't carrying any dive equipment, but he didn't question them. Instead, he said, "Welcome aboard. You've brought beautiful weather for the first of October."

Liam's first mate and sole crew member was another sun-tanned Aussie, who came up from below. "Coop, Zoe, this is my main man, Rich," Liam said.

Rich offered his hand to Zoe and hoisted her aboard. "It's good to meet ya, folks." Coop hopped onboard and Liam followed.

Liam pointed to the bridge. "I'm going to finish checking the instruments. You guys make yourselves at home." Zoe followed Rich into the cabin. Coop hung around on deck.

Coop climbed the five stairs leading to the flybridge. Liam was checking a list and flipping switches. Coop handed him a piece of paper. "These are the coordinates."

Liam looked at the paper and began punching numbers into the GPS. When he finished, he tapped ENTER and a bright orange line appeared on the screen. It began at the shoreline where they were docked and ended in the middle of the ocean. He turned to Coop. "Hey, man, look at this. You can't dive out there, it's way too deep."

"We'll check it out when we get there," Coop said. "It's getting late. We better get going."

"Whatever...it's your money."

Coop hung around the bridge as Liam motored out of the harbor and into open sea. Once clear, Liam accelerated to cruise power and checked the bearing on the GPS. It read one hundred and eighty-three degrees. He flipped on the autopilot and set a heading of 183. The boat appeared as a blue circle on the orange line. "Looking good," Liam said.

"Want kind of speed are we getting?" Coop asked.

Liam looked at the instruments. "We're showing twenty-four knots, but we have a three-knot wind coming straight at our bow, so we're only doing twenty-one through the water."

"What's that in English?"

Liam laughed as he pulled out a hand instrument that resembled an old slide rule. He lined up a couple numbers. "Twenty-four miles an hour." He glanced at the autopilot. "It looks like we'll be at your sunken sub in twelve hours and thirty-one minutes." Coop looked at his watch. It was almost 2:00 p.m.

"I doubt you'll do much diving at two-thirty in the morning," Liam said.

"We'll get up bright and early tomorrow."

Liam mumbled under his breath. "Yeah, bright and early."

"Hey, you got anything for lunch?" Coop asked.

"Head on down to the galley. Rich is making sandwiches. I'll be there as soon as this baby settles in."

Coop looked around the cabin. It was surprisingly plush for a diving boat. It had two couches separated by a coffee table, a couple of lamps and an area rug. The galley was appointed with stainless steel: built-in cook-top, microwave, and refrigerator. Rich was smearing the last coat of mayonnaise on some baloney sandwiches.

"Need any help?" Coop asked.

"No thanks, I'm good at these. My mama fed them to me every day for fifteen years."

"Pretty tough growing up in Australia?" Zoe asked.

"My dad was a hand on a commercial fishing trawler. He'd work his ass off for two weeks and come home with four or five pineapples."

"Pineapples?"

Rich laughed. "Oh, sorry, that's Aussie for fifty-dollar bills." He put out the sandwiches and opened a large bag of chips. "The best day of my life was when I met Liam. He's a good man. I've got a pretty nice life out here in the Cocos."

Liam had quietly entered the cabin. "Oh, God, not baloney again." He opened the fridge. "Anyone for a beer?"

The sea was relatively calm and created little roll to the boat as it cut through the water. "The winds are dying down." Liam said. "We should get to where we're going before two." He looked at Zoe, "Coop says he can't wait till tomorrow when you guys dive on that sub."

Zoe took a big bite from her sandwich. "Any mustard?"

The sun set a little before seven off the starboard side. Liam returned to the bridge to check the instruments and calculate the fuel burn and, while he was there, turned on the running lights and the interior cabin lights. Rich prepared another one of Mama's recipes: fried fish, fried potatoes and fried onions. After dinner Coop and Zoe took over a couple of bunk beds to get some rest.

When Coop awoke, he was drenched in sweat. He changed his shirt and checked the bunk above him. Zoe was still asleep. He looked at the boat's bell clock; it was 11:35 p.m. He quietly opened their duffel, took out the bottle of Jack and made his way up to the deck where Liam was leaning against a guardrail, smoking a cigarette. "Got another one of those?" Coop asked.

Liam turned around and tapped the pack; a couple of cigarettes popped out. Coop took one and Liam snapped his lighter. Coop took a drag, coughed twice and let smoke out through his nostrils. "It's really peaceful," he said.

Liam looked off into space. "I could never go back to the city."

Coop took another hit off his cigarette then flicked it into the ocean. He opened the bottle of sour mash and handed it to Liam. "Are you allowed?"

Liam took a generous swig. "I'm thinking I may need this."

"Yeah? Why's that?"

"Come on, Coop, it's obvious you're not divers and I know there's no sunken sub, so who the hell are you guys?"

Coop swallowed a mouthful of the amber colored liquor. "I was gonna tell you when the time was right."

"How about right now?"

"Another drink?" Coop asked.

"That bad, huh?"

"We're U.S. agents."

Liam smirked. "That's no big surprise, but why are we headed to the middle of the ocean?"

"There's an island out there."

Liam shook his head. "An island? I don't think so."

"Trust me, there is."

"So, what's on this invisible island?

"I'm not sure, but I'll know soon enough."

Liam lit another cigarette and offered one to Coop, but he declined. The only sound came from the twin diesels that were chugging away in sync with each other. Liam finished his smoke and locked eyes with Coop. "Look, man, I did a lot of dangerous shit when I was young. I had nothin' to lose then, but now I have this boat. I can't risk losing her."

"Trust me, you're not going to lose her."

"Trust you? I dunno—some kind of spy mission to the middle of nowhere? I don't have a good feeling about this."

"Look, Liam, Zoe and I have been through this drill before. We're good at our jobs and we're good at protecting our team."

Liam's eyes narrowed. "Your team? We didn't sign up to be part of your team."

"I get that, but what I'm saying is that I'm not going to put you or Rich, or your boat, at risk."

"You've already put us at risk." He pulled away from the rail and started for the flybridge.

Coop grabbed his arm. "Where are you going?"

He pushed Coop's hand away. "This just doesn't feel right." He brushed by Coop and took two steps at a time to the bridge.

Coop steadied himself against the guardrail as the boat did an aggressive one-eighty. He took another slug from the Jack Daniels, twisted the cap back on and slowly mounted the steps to the flybridge. Liam was busy re-programming the GPS. He knew

Coop was there, but he didn't acknowledge him. "Tell me I didn't pick the wrong guy," Coop said.

Liam wouldn't make eye contact. "I'm sorry, man, but I didn't know what I was getting into."

"What are you talking about? You just said you knew we weren't divers. Did you think this was a sightseeing trip?"

"I don't know what I thought, but it wasn't this. I'll give you your deposit back. The fuel is on me." Liam advanced the throttles.

Coop waited until the boat was back at cruise power and enough time had passed for Liam to settle down. "What's your monthly payment on this rig?" Coop asked.

"Twenty-one hundred and change. Why?"

"Can you really afford to throw away five-grand? That's almost three payments."

"No, I can't, but I can't afford to lose this boat either."

"Listen, pull those throttles back for a minute so we can talk." Liam looked down at the deck where Rich and Zoe were staring up at the bridge trying to figure out what was going on. He retarded both engines to idle and turned to face Coop.

"You don't have to go to the island," Coop said. "You can anchor a safe distance offshore and Zoe and I will take the dinghy the rest of the way."

Liam hesitated. "I dunno."

Coop put his hand on Liam's shoulder. "Liam, give us three hours, just three. If we're not back, you can leave without us."

"I couldn't do that."

"You sure could if that's our deal and I'm willing to make that deal. So, what d'ya say?"

He mulled over Coop's proposal. "I'm putting Rich's ass on the line here, too," he said. "I've gotta let him in on it." He descended from the bridge to the main deck where Rich and Zoe had been observing the confrontation. Zoe saw what was coming and excused herself for a visit to the head.

Liam huddled for five minutes with his first mate. Rich nodded several times and then the two men shook hands. Liam returned to the bridge and walked right past Coop. He spun the control wheel in a circle and advanced the throttles. "Three hours," he said.

Forty-one

Coop looked at his watch. It was almost one o'clock. He turned to Zoe, "Go get dressed, I'll be down in a couple of minutes." Zoe disappeared into the main cabin. Coop waited five minutes and joined her. She had on a pair of nylon running shorts, a bathing suit top and a pair of the water shoes they had acquired from the supply store. While Coop was changing his clothes, Zoe stuffed a scarf, T-shirt, flashlight, and her Glock and shoulder holster into the waterproof fanny pack. Coop put on a similar outfit, but left his upper half bare; the outside air was a comfortable eighty-two degrees. He stuffed his fanny pack with the same items as Zoe's.

Liam was at the helm keeping a keen eye out for any signs of the mysterious island that Coop was so obsessed with discovering. Coop and Zoe joined him on the bridge. "Any binoculars?" Coop asked. Liam opened a cabinet and handed a pair to each of them.

The GPS showed the destination at twenty-two miles dead ahead. Zoe took the left quadrant and Coop the right. As the GPS hit the eight-mile mark, Zoe said, "Coop, bingo at ten o'clock."

Coop swung his binoculars to the left. A faint glimmer of lights was perceptible. He turned to Liam. "Slow it down and turn ten right...and cut all the lights." Liam followed instructions and crept forward at four knots. The lights kept getting brighter until they could be seen by the naked eye. "How far to shore?" Coop asked.

Liam checked the GPS. "About two and a quarter miles."

"Are you good with dropping anchor out here?" Coop asked. Liam raised his thumb. "Then cut the engines," Coop said.

Except for the lapping of water against the hull, it was dead still. Coop broke the silence. "Okay, this is it. Drop the dinghy off the stern."

Liam and Rich let out slack on the tie-down ropes and the rubber raft dropped onto the water. Liam held a large flashlight, and Rich, who was stripped down to a swimsuit, jumped in the water and crawled into the dinghy. There was dive equipment strewn all over the raft. Rich shoved the wet suits and masks into one end and the tanks and spearguns into the other. He shouted up at Coop, "Will this stuff be in your way? "

"No problem, we'll work around it," Coop said. He looked at Zoe. "Your turn." She jumped into the water. Coop turned to Liam. "It's one-thirty. If we're not back by four-thirty ... you know what to do."

"Yeah, I know."

Coop dropped into the water. Rich lent them a hand into the dinghy and then proceeded to provide them with the Readers Digest version of the operating manual. "The engine's electric, so it's silent. It's charged to the max—good for three hours of use. The green button turns it on, the red one turns it off. Throttle's on the tiller like any other outboard. Any questions?"

"We're good. Thanks, buddy," Coop said.

Rich clasped Coop's hand and squeezed. "Good luck, man." He turned to Zoe and gave her a hug. "Take care of this guy, will ya?"

"That's a chore, he's a guy and guys just don't listen."

He laughed, "I get it. That's what my girlfriend always says." He jumped back into the water and swam toward a ladder on the port side. Coop pushed the green button, turned the throttle and the dinghy disappeared into the darkness.

The waters that were calm two miles out turned into high waves as the dinghy approached the shore. When they were close enough to stand, Coop and Zoe jumped out and hauled on the lead rope to drag the dinghy ashore. The white caps attacked—knocking them off their feet. They got up, tugged again on the rope and the dinghy slowly escaped the wrath of the waves. When it was safely on the beach, they flopped face-up on the sand. Zoe was breathing heavily, but Coop was sucking for all the air he could get.

They didn't have the luxury of resting very long. Coop's internal radar came alive. He stood and surveyed the beach. Through the pitch darkness, not far up the beach, he recognized the glow of cigarettes. "Zoe, get up," he said. She rose to her knees. Coop pointed and Zoe spotted the flickering orange dots.

They dragged the dinghy toward the underbrush that connected the sand to the forest and shoved it under the dense bushes. They took their pistols from their fanny packs and crawled in next to the raft.

The orange dots came closer and the sound of two voices became louder. Coop and Zoe peered out from the bushes. Two men wearing shorts and military shirts and carrying Uzis over their shoulders came into view. They were speaking a language neither Coop nor Zoe understood, and they were patrolling the beach with a nonchalance that comes when one isn't really expecting intruders.

The men passed within two feet of Coop and Zoe, but continued down the beach talking and laughing; their voices quickly faded. Coop and Zoe crawled out of hiding. "Who were they?" Zoe asked.

"It looked like their shirts had the red and green Iranian flag on them."

"Iran? Are you sure?"

"Pretty sure. And it sounded like they were speaking Farsi."

"What the hell are they doing here?"

"I dunno. We'll find out."

They removed the contents from their fanny packs and put on dry T-shirts and head-scarves, then strapped their holsters over their shoulders and secured their Glocks. They turned on their flashlights and trudged into the forest.

The going was slow. There was no path leading inland and the brush was thick and gnarly. Coop cursed at himself for not bringing a machete or some other tool that could cut through the vegetation, but it was too late to second guess that decision. Their bare legs were being scratched and gouged, but they plodded forward.

The underbrush began to thin and they came upon an area where the bushes had been cut away. It had the semblance of a path and it appeared to be leading somewhere. They were able to move on more quickly and then, abruptly, they stepped into a clearing.

Coop sprayed the beam from his flashlight across the clearing. Fifteen yards to the right a long stretch of firmly packed crushed coral, resembling a wide road, extended straight ahead well beyond the range of his light. Piled on the near end of the road, at least twenty feet high, was a huge mound of cut branches and leaves. Coop pointed to the pile. "What d'ya think that is?"

They approached the pile and as they got closer it became obvious the pyramid of cut foliage was more than just a mass of debris. They focused their lights on the mound. Under the debris they could see their beams reflecting off silver metal. Coop pulled at a branch and jumped out of the way as a load of brown and green vegetation came tumbling down. A dozen plexiglass windows appeared through the void.

He turned to Zoe, "Give me a hand." The two of them tugged and yanked on a large limb until they wrenched it free, creating another avalanche of dead leaves and boughs. They gaped at what they had uncovered—the fuselage of an airliner with a portable ladder leading to an open passenger door. Coop ran his beam across the fuselage. It stopped on the logo—a world globe with the name *Burma Air* in the center.

Zoe appeared mesmerized, almost as though she couldn't believe what she was looking at. She snapped out of it and said, "I'll be damned. It's actually here."

"It's here all right," Coop said. "I'm just trying to figure out what those Iranian soldiers are doing here."

"If the plane is here, then the gold is here, too. They must be guarding it," Zoe said.

"From whom? And why bring it to this desolate place? It just doesn't make sense."

The sound of a door slamming echoed through the still night air. Coop and Zoe turned off their flashlights and gazed in the direction of the sound. On the other side of the clearing they could make out a cluster of lights. "The ones we saw from the boat," Zoe said.

"Yeah, let's take a look." Coop unholstered his Glock and Zoe did the same as they inched toward the lights. Twenty yards from the source, Coop put up his hand. The lights were radiating from a group of buildings. There were close to a dozen Quonset huts positioned in a semicircle and in the center was a large unpainted industrial building with a roof covered in a checkerboard of pipes and a cluster of exhaust stacks.

Coop pointed to the closest hut. They crept toward it. There was no glass in the windows frames—only screens to keep the bugs out. Coop snuck up on one of the them and peered in. Men were asleep in bunks—most were snoring and snorting. Their clothes, along with several white lab coats, were hanging on pegs.

He motioned for Zoe to take a look. She took a step forward, but her shoe caught in a hole and she went down with a thud. One of the sleepers awoke and jumped out of bed. Coop grabbed Zoe's shoulder and pulled her out of the light and out of sight. They crouched behind a supply shed. The door of the hut opened and a bearded man headed straight for them. Coop raised his pistol. The man stopped short of the shed and emptied his bladder.

They allowed ten minutes for the man to get back to sleep before they ventured from their hiding spot. Coop led the way, circumventing the next three huts to get them into position for surveillance of the large building.

Two soldiers, maybe the same ones they saw on the beach, were outside the building smoking and laughing. One flicked his cigarette into the dirt, slapped the other guy on the back and strolled off toward a Quonset hut. The remaining soldier settled into a lawn chair stationed next to the building's front door. He laid his Uzi across his lap and within five minutes he was fast asleep.

They pounced. Zoe grabbed the Uzi and Coop shoved his pistol against the man's temple. His eyes opened in bewilderment to meet Coop's icy stare. Coop held his finger to his lips, but in spite of the warning the guard began to babble away in Farsi. Zoe removed her scarf and wrapped it around his mouth. Coop forced the man to his feet and nudged him toward the door. Zoe pointed to the placard on the front—the international symbol for radioactive material. "Yeah, I saw it," Coop said." He dug into the guard's pocket, came up with a set of keys and tossed them to Zoe. She unlocked the door.

Coop shoved the guard inside and Zoe followed. Their jaws dropped. The interior was one huge room with a ceiling reaching at least twenty feet. The contents were a maze of stainless steel canisters, vats and pipes. Computers, all humming in unison, were lined up along the near wall. The far wall was totally dedicated to digital timers that flashed on and off, with constantly changing readouts.

"What the hell's going on in here?" Zoe asked.

"Not quite sure, but we're not leaving 'til we find out." He spotted several rolls of duct tape on a work table and used them to lash the guard to a chair.

He picked up a pile of papers from a nearby desk. They contained rows and rows of numbers with narratives written in Arabic. Several dozen clipboards, covered with graphs, lay next to them. "See what you can find in the back. I'll check around here," Coop said.

Zoe reached the far wall where she spotted dozens of sealed barrels stacked one on top of the other. Alongside were a half dozen empties. She extended her arm inside the nearest empty and rolled her finger across its sides. She shouted, "Coop, back here."

He came running. "What d'ya have?"

Zoe held up her finger. It was covered with brownish-yellow powder. "The warehouse."

Coop swept his finger across the inside of the barrel to collect a good sample. He rubbed the powdery stuff between his thumb and forefinger, smelled it and dabbed it on his tongue; he made a face and spit it out. Then, like a bolt of lightning, it struck him and a wide grin spread across his face.

"What?" Zoe said.

"Son of a bitch. Now, I remember what this is. It's Yellowcake."

"Yellow what?"

Coop spat on the floor again, trying to free his mouth of the bitter substance. "Yellowcake. It can be turned into fuel for nuclear reactors. We found tons of this stuff in Iraq, but all of it was supposed to have been shipped off to Canada."

"So they're making nuclear fuel here?"

"Not a bad place for it if you want to keep it a secret."

"What about the gold?"

"What gold?"

"Saddam's gold—the stuff we've been looking for. You do remember, don't you?"

"Yeah, I remember, but it looks like there never was any gold. This must be what Saddam really hid."

"Shit, no wonder there are Iranian soldiers all over this place. Coop, we can't take them on. We gotta get out of here."

Coop ran his hand through his hair. "Yeah, let me think for a minute."

Forty-two

Coop checked to make sure the guard was still securely taped to the chair before he opened the door a crack and peered out. The compound's inhabitants were still asleep. He gave Zoe a nod and they scurried out and slipped into the shadows on the edge of the clearing. Coop looked at his watch; it was 3:36. "We can make it. Get the dinghy ready and I'll be there by ten after four."

"That's cutting it pretty close. You told Liam to leave at four-thirty."

"I'll be there in time. You just have the dinghy launched with the motor running," Coop said.

She wasted no time and took off into the forest. Coop broke into a sprint to cross the clearing, but he began sucking air again and sat down to catch his breath. He coughed a few times, rose to his feet and jogged the rest of the way.

One or two branches of camouflage still covered the bottom of the ladder. Coop tugged on the biggest one to gain access to the steps and climbed quickly into the plane. Inside, the combination of a waning moon and obstructed windows created total darkness.

He turned on his flashlight and sprayed the beam across the seats. He was in the first-class section.

Coop made his way along the aisle, passing eight rows of leather cushions and a forward galley. He opened the door to the cockpit. It wasn't totally unfamiliar. His dad flew a twin-engine Beechcraft and when he was young, Coop spent hundreds of hours in the right seat next to him.

The cockpit was covered with instruments, overhead toggles and panel push buttons. Coop did a quick scan, but ignored most of what he saw. He zeroed in on three buttons:

BATTERY POWER, ENGINE #1, ENGINE #2. He depressed the battery power button. The panel lights flickered green, then red, then green again.

He was relieved there was enough electrical power to light the instrument panel, but that didn't mean there was enough juice to power the starter. He pushed the button marked ENGINE #1. A backfire with the decibel level of a small cannon interrupted the night's silence. Coop looked through the side window; smoke was rising from the back of the left engine cowling.

The huts lit up and the compound came alive. Soldiers and scientists poured from the barracks pointing fingers toward the plane. Coop made another attempt at ENGINE #1. This time there was nothing—just silence. He looked out the side window; soldiers were running in his direction. He desperately scanned the panel again and this time spotted a button marked AUXILIARY POWER UNIT. He pushed it and heard a motor start near the back of the airplane. A solid green light appeared. He depressed the ENGINE #1 button for a third time and this time the left engine roared to life. He peered out the window again; soldiers were only a few yards away. He quickly pushed the ENGINE #2 button and to his relief the right engine began to hum.

The soldiers reached the plane and were scrambling up the stairs of the ladder. Coop advanced the throttles. As the plane moved forward the ladder toppled and the soldiers were splattered across the ground. Coop pushed hard on the left rudder, directing the plane to veer off the runway at a ninety-degree angle. The nuclear facility was at twelve o'clock, two-hundred yards away.

Soldiers opened fire on the plane. Bullets pierced the plexiglass and passed through the cockpit's aluminum ceiling. Coop ducked below the window line and used both feet to depress the brakes as he advanced the throttles full forward. He listened for the sound of the engines spooling up. When he felt they were at full power, he released the brakes, leaped from the seat and made a mad dash out of the cockpit.

He could feel the plane accelerating and he could hear a loudspeaker blaring: "exit door open...exit door open..." He reached the open door and yanked a red handle. Immediately, the emergency evacuation slide deployed and Coop jumped into the nylon chute. The forward inertia of the plane shot him down the slide and he hit the ground hard just as the left wing passed overhead. Eight seconds later the Airbus 320 impacted the nuclear facility.

The explosion was mammoth. A plume of smoke rose fifty feet in the air and flames erupted everywhere. Bodies were strewn across the ground and those who were still alive were desperately crawling away from the scene. The forest that bordered the compound began to crackle as underbrush ignited and the fire gained in strength and intensity.

Coop propped himself up, inhaled a dose of burning jet fuel and looked around. In the middle of the chaos, no one was paying attention to him. He crawled toward the path leading to the beach and once out of sight, he took an inventory of his injuries. He had several cuts and bruises, but he was most concerned about his left shoulder. He had trouble moving his arm and blood was oozing through the left side of his T-shirt. He cradled his left arm in his right and pushed through the forest toward the water.

His flashlight was gone, making it impossible to see the sharp edges of the underbrush. Spikes tore at his skin, turning his arms and legs red. Eventually, he could hear the sound of the waves lapping against the shore; a few minutes later he emerged from the forest. He looked around the beach. The dinghy was removed from the underbrush and was sitting near the water. The pile of diving equipment Rich had arranged so neatly in the corners of the raft was strewn across the sand. There was no sign of Zoe. Coop heard someone coming through the forest behind him. He reached for his Glock. His holster was empty.

~ * ~

Liam and Rich stared in the direction of the island. Red and orange flames raced toward the sky and the fire's ferocity was building every second. Liam looked at his watch. It was 4:25.

"Should I start the engines?" Rich asked.

"Wait a couple of minutes," Liam said.

"It's almost four-thirty."

"I know, but they'll burn to death on that island."

"Boss, they're probably dead already. If we don't get out of here, we may be too."

Liam looked again at his watch and banged his fist against the railing. "Damn it. Okay, start 'em."

Forty-three

It took all Coop's strength to push the dinghy into the water with only one arm. He started to climb in when a voice yelled, "hold it." Coop turned around. Marco was gripping a gun in one hand and a duffel in the other. Flames were licking at the bushes behind him. He pointed his pistol at Coop. "Hold it right there, I'm going with you."

"Going where?"

Marco pointed out to sea. "You've got a boat out there... somewhere. Let's go."

Coop looked at his watch; it was 4:37. "It's too late. It left at four-thirty."

Marco tossed his duffel into the dinghy. "Without their hero? I doubt that. Get in and let's get out of here."

Coop managed to climb into the raft and took a seat in the rear next to the motor. Marco sat in the front next to his canvas bag and looked back toward the beach. The flames were dropping embers onto the edge of the sand. "Start that motherfucker and get going," he said.

Coop pushed the green button and the motor began to hum. "We can get away from the island, but I'm telling you the boat is gone."

Marco pointed his pistol at Coop. "Take me to that fuckin' boat or I'll blow your head off." Coop motored away from the raging blaze and into the darkness of the ocean.

When they were a safe distance from shore, Marco took out a flashlight, pointed it out to sea and flicked it on and off...on and off... Out of the darkness, several hundred yards ahead, a spotlight flashed and swept across the water. Marco snickered. "Well, well, what do you know?" He pointed his Glock at Coop. "Get out."

Coop brought the motor to idle. "What d'ya mean, out?"

"Or I can shoot you in the middle of the forehead, like I did Ghazali. It's your choice."

Coop slid his legs over the side and dropped into the water. Marco tucked the pistol under his belt and settled into the vacant seat near the motor. He peered in the direction of the light source and reached for the accelerator. From behind the dinghy, a harpoon caught Marco between the shoulder blades; it passed through his midsection and protruded out the front of his chest. He listed to the side and tumbled into the water.

A voice from behind said, "How goes it, boss?"

Coop turned. Zoe was wearing diving gear and holding a speargun.

"Goin' pretty good now. You get to Liam?"

"Yeah, just before he took off."

"Good work. What d'ya say we get outa this water?"

"For sure. It feels like it's starting to boil."

They crawled into the dinghy and Zoe peeled off the scuba gear. She pointed to the duffel. "Is that filled with what I think it is?"

"Open it," Coop said.

Zoe unfastened the zipper and spread the sides of the canvas bag. It was stuffed with bundles of cash.

The dinghy pulled alongside Liam's boat. The pungent aroma of diesel exhaust never smelled so sweet. Rich jumped into the water and secured the ropes to bring the raft back on deck, while Liam gave Coop and Zoe a hand coming aboard. He noticed the heavy duffel, but he didn't ask about it. Coop winced when Liam grabbed his arm. "That shoulder looks nasty," Liam said.

"Nothing's broken, I'll be fine. Thanks for waiting."

"It was close. I was on the bridge with my hands on the throttles when Zoe got here." Liam took out a pack of cigarettes and handed one to Coop.

Coop hesitated, but took it anyway. Liam snapped his lighter and Coop deeply inhaled. He took one puff and threw the cigarette into the water. "Guess I'm out of shape," he said.

Liam nodded and looked back at the island. The entire three-square miles were engulfed in flames. "Nobody's going to survive that," he said. "You want to tell me what happened?"

"Better you don't know," Coop said.

Liam didn't press any further and turned his attention to Rich's work. The dinghy was aboard and tethered. "I'm going to get us out of here," he said. "Hey, I turned on the water heater; you guys look like you can use a shower." He climbed the stairs to the flybridge and Coop and Zoe went below.

"Are you okay?" Zoe asked.

"Yeah, just a little beaten up. That's all."

"You sure, that's all?"

"I'm sure."

They returned to the deck after a hot shower and a change of clothes. The boat was heading away from the island on autopilot and Liam and Rich were sharing drinks from the bottle of Jack Daniels. Rich lifted two glasses and handed them to Coop and Zoe. "You guys probably need these."

The four of them sat in silence sipping the liquor and watching the orange ball get smaller and smaller as the boat headed back to the Cocos.

It was almost three in the afternoon when the pier came into view. Liam motored in and reversed the engines when the boat neared the pier. The bow nudged against the rubber bumpers hanging from the dock, and Rich secured the tie-down ropes. "That was one hell of a diving trip," Liam said.

Coop laughed, slapped Liam on the back and handed him a roll of hundred-dollar bills. "And you're one hell of a captain."

Zoe gave Rich a kiss on the cheek. "Thanks, Rich. Don't ever leave the Cocos, this is where you belong."

Forty-four

Coop carried the duffel full of cash with his good arm and Zoe threw the one containing their personal things over her shoulder. They hoofed it to the airport.

"Do you have any money left?" Zoe asked.

"Not much," Coop said.

"How much is not much?"

"About twelve hundred."

"How were you planning to get us home?"

"I was hoping you'd charge the tickets on your card and I'd pay you back later."

"Are you good for it?"

"Trust me, I'll pay you back." Zoe broke out laughing. "Did I say something funny?" Coop asked.

"No, but apparently the irony is lost on you. You're carrying millions of dollars in that bag, but you don't have enough cash to buy us plane tickets home."

Coop patted the duffel like it was a new puppy. "I wish it were mine, but it's not."

"Whose is it?"

"That's a good question, but I know it's not mine."

The fastest way home was a Burma Airlines flight to Istanbul followed by a Turkish Airlines to D.C. and as promised, Zoe charged the flight on her Visa card. The layover in Istanbul, two and a half hours, wasn't enough time to nap, but it was plenty of time to nurse a couple of beers. "What do I owe you?" Coop asked.

"Counting the flight from Damascus to the Cocos?"

"Shit, I forgot about those. Yeah, what's the bottom line?"

"Eighty-eight hundred and change."

The bar had a display rack of postcards touting various tourist destinations. Coop recognized one and grabbed it from the rack. It had a picture of the ocean and a girl in a bikini, along with the caption, HAVING FUN IN THE COCOS. He borrowed a red pen from the bartender and jotted a note on the back of it: *Craig Cooper owes Zoe Fields $8,800.*

"My marker," he said. "Due and payable when we get back." Zoe laughed and stuffed the postcard into her pocket.

By the time Coop and Zoe boarded the Turkish Airlines flight to D.C., they had gone without sleep for twenty-five hours. Luckily a seat was empty between them; they stretched out and slept through the first half of the twelve-hour flight.

The clanking of plates and the popping of soda cans woke them. "I'm starved," Zoe said. "Can we afford a Scotch with our Chateaubriand?"

"You mean with our rubber chicken. Go for it...I'll have one too."

They were both wrong—it was lasagna. Zoe wolfed it down and ordered another Scotch. "How much do you think is in the duffel?" she asked.

"Should be nine million."

"Iran's final payment for the Yellowcake?"

"Yeah, including the broker's commission."

Zoe thought about her talk with Lara. She hoped Lara had taken her advice and headed back to Zurich when the commission hadn't shown up.

The flight attendant brought Zoe a miniature bottle of Johnny Walker. She poured half into her glass and emptied the rest into Coop's. They sipped their drinks without any conversation. Zoe was the first to speak, "Something's bothering you, Coop."

"You mean other than blowing up an island with fifty people on it?"

"That was your job. I'm talking about your personal life?"

Coop squeezed the last drop from his glass. "It's a mess. Fran got a divorce attorney."

"Oh, I'm sorry. Anything I can do? Maybe you can crash at my place when we get back?"

"Thanks, but you don't need me hanging around. I come with more baggage than just a duffel full of money."

"Hey, you're not the first guy I know who's gone through a divorce."

Coop fiddled with his fork and shoved the remainder of his lasagna around with some uneaten broccoli. "Can I confide?"

"Always. You know that."

"I...I found out I have lung cancer."

Zoe closed her eyes and sighed. "When?"

"The doctor called me the day before we left on the assignment."

"How bad?"

"I don't know. The doc wanted me to start treatment, but I told him I had to wait 'til I got back."

"So, you'll get in touch tomorrow?"

"I'll call him when we settle this whole mess."

"But Coop..."

"Listen, there's a shit storm brewing and I have to make sure Fran and Josh are taken care of and..."

"And what."

"I have to make sure you come out of this thing okay."

Zoe put her hand on Coop's cheek. "Don't worry about me. You know I've always been able to look out for myself."

He squeezed her hand. "Well, I'm going to make sure. After all, you have my marker for eighty-eight hundred dollars." Zoe laughed.

The flight attendant took away the dinner dishes and set a chocolate something in front of each of them. Coop turned to Zoe. "Where did you disappear to the night before we got on the boat?"

"What? Oh, I went for a walk to shake off the nerves."

Coop dug into the gooey dessert. It looked good, but looks were deceiving. He made a face and dropped his napkin into the dish. "Did you meet the blonde?"

Zoe's stared straight ahead. "Blonde? What blonde?"

"The one in the bar. That was Lara, wasn't it?"

"You'd make a good spy. Ever think of that line of work?"

He laughed. "No way, too dangerous. You want to talk about it?"

Zoe sighed and recounted the whole story: the bar, the ladies' room, the Windsurfer hotel, the broker commission pickup, and Lara's desire to talk about their future together. She finished by saying, "Sorry, I should have told you."

"It's okay, it wouldn't have changed our mission. What d'ya think, though? Is there a future for you with Lara?"

Zoe shrugged. "I know this sounds crazy, but I think she may be the one."

"Really? So you're going to pursue it?"

"Maybe. I'd like to, but we'll see."

"What d'ya mean, we'll see?"

"I said I'd call her and I really want to. I've been looking for someone for a long time, but my experience with long-distance relationships is that they never work."

"Look, you want some advice?"

"I know you. I'm going to get it whether I want it or not."

"Call her. Call her when we get back to the States. Take it from somebody who had to learn it the hard way...the older you get, the faster life speeds by."

Zoe thought for a moment. "I appreciate the advice, but I just don't think it will work."

Coop turned Zoe's head and stared directly into her eyes. "I know you. If you want something bad enough, you'll find a way to make it happen. Come on, Zoe, make it happen."

She planted a kiss on Coop's forehead. "Thanks, boss, I'll think about it. If I can figure out a way...a way to really make it work, I'll call her."

The combination of sleep deprivation and two ounces of alcohol went to work on her central nervous system. Zoe yawned, leaned her head onto Coop's shoulder and dropped off to sleep.

Forty-five

Randy wasn't intimidated by many people, but Director Dutton was definitely one of them. A phone conversation would have suited Randy, but 'the man' wanted a face-to-face. Randy paced back and forth in the reception room until he was summoned into the director's private office.

Dutton was only five-foot-ten, two inches shorter than Randy, but Randy always felt he was looking up at him.

"I don't bite. Sit down, relax," the director said.

Randy settled into a chair facing the director's desk. "Thank you, sir."

"Coffee, water, something hard?"

"No, I'm fine, thanks."

Dutton tapped the top of his pen on the desk. "So, tell me. How's the gold operation going?"

Randy's left eye twitched. "Not good. Coop's chasing his tail over there. I think I should bring him home."

"Really?"

"Yeah, the operation was closed for ten months. That was way too long. The gold's disappeared."

"Cooper's only been there for a couple of weeks. Maybe you should let him dig a little more."

"He told me he struck out."

"Huh, that doesn't sound like Cooper."

"What can I say?"

"He couldn't find any leads at all?"

"None. I'm asking your permission to bring him home."

"Maybe another agent?"

"Sir, face it. The gold's disappeared. It's gone."

The director grimaced and leaned back in his chair, clasping his hands behind his head. "Okay, follow your gut. Close it down."

Randy wasn't sure if he should apologize or thank him, so he did neither.

"I was wondering, did you send that guy Torelli along with Cooper?" Dutton asked.

"No, why?"

"An Australian cutter was investigating an island on fire in the Indian Ocean. It was so hot they couldn't get very close, but they found a body floating offshore."

"I don't understand," Randy said.

"The floater had Agency credentials. It was your guy, Marco Torelli."

"Marco? Dead? Are you sure?"

"Of course, I'm sure. What was he doing way out there anyway?"

Randy's left eye twitched. "I don't know. He was digging into a money-laundering scheme out of Sydney, but the last I heard he was on his way home."

"Well, you better send a couple of people over there. Sorry about your guy."

"Yeah, thanks, I'll take care of it. If there's nothing else..." The director stood and offered his hand. Randy did the same.

Randy started for the door, but Dutton raised a finger, "and Randy..."

He turned around. "Sir?"

"Have Cooper stop by when he gets back. I want to debrief him."

"Will do," Randy said. He left the director's office and hastened his step. He needed to get back to his office and make some calls, and needed to make them right away.

Forty-six

Coop and Zoe deplaned together, but as they approached the Customs station, Zoe laid back and waited for the end of the line. Coop stood patiently as the Customs agent searched the luggage of a housewife whom he caught trying to smuggle in four watches by wearing all of them on the same wrist. When his turn arrived, Coop handed the Customs officer his Victor Special. The agent examined the passport. "Mr. Hayes, what was the purpose of your visits to Iraq and Turkey and Syria?"

"I write, I'm a journalist."

"Newspapers or magazines?"

"I freelance."

The agent flipped the passport's pages. "I see you were in the Cocos. There's not much to write about out there."

"You got that right, I was fishing. Great Bluefin."

The agent pointed to Coop's duffel. "Let's have a look."

Coop opened the bag and turned it upside down. A pile of dirty clothes and a bunch of toiletries spilled onto the counter. The agent wrinkled his nose and stamped Coop's passport. "Next."

Zoe waved people ahead so that when her turn arrived, she was alone with the customs agent. Zoe flashed her ID, passport and gold badge. "I'm a U.S. agent."

The Customs officer examined her credentials, then pointed to the duffel. "Are you bringing anything in?"

"You could say that."

"Open your case, ma'am."

"No."

"I'm telling you to open your case."

"And I'm telling you not to get involved in Agency business."

The Customs agent struggled to regain control. He opened the zipper himself and spread the sides of the duffel; several bundles of hundred-dollar bills spilled out. "Whoa, why are you carrying all this cash?"

Zoe's eyes could have pierced metal. "You know better than to ask me that."

The agent was caught off guard. "But this is a lot of money..."

She tossed the loose bundles back into the duffel. "It's none of your concern. Do your job and stay out of the way of mine."

The agent opened Zoe's passport again and went through the motions of re-examining it. "Maybe I should make a phone call," he said.

"That's up to you, but just have your badge number handy when the Agency director calls you back."

The two agents had a stare-down, but the customs guy blinked first. He stamped Zoe's passport. "Welcome back, Agent Fields." Zoe zipped up the duffel, dragged it off the table and walked toward the exit. The Customs agent picked up his phone and tapped in some numbers. "The woman has it," he said.

Zoe blended in with the throng of people, all in a hurry to get somewhere else. She spotted a restroom with the universal symbols: MALE, FEMALE, HANDICAPPED. She pushed open the door and slipped inside. Five minutes later, she came out and was met by two of her least favorite co-workers: Dorsey, a two-faced dick who climbed the Agency ladder on the backs of his colleagues, and his sidekick Noonan, a jerk who most likely had a hard time passing the Agency's IQ test.

Dorsey relieved Zoe of her duffel and Noonan grabbed her arm. "Let's go," he said.

"What, not even a hello?"

Noonan couldn't contain his contempt. "Don't hold your breath. It beats me why they even let chicks like you into the Agency."

Zoe rammed her knee into Noonan's crotch. "That's why, you prick."

Noonan doubled over until the pain that radiated from his testicles into his stomach had subsided, then he came at Zoe with a vengeance. Dorsey wedged himself between them. "That's enough. Noonan, pick up the duffel." Noonan did as he was told. He tried to act as if he wasn't hurting, but he had trouble standing upright.

Dorsey pointed to an unmarked door. "This'll do." A clerk sitting behind a metal desk looked up in surprise. Dorsey flashed his badge. "How 'bout you take a short coffee break." The clerk was noticeably annoyed, but respected the badge and left the room.

Noonan unzipped the duffel and emptied it on the desk. Dirty clothes and loose toiletries spilled out. He stared at Zoe. "Where's the fuckin' money?"

"If you didn't have your head up your ass you'd already know," Zoe said.

Noonan lunged at her. "You arrogant bitch."

Dorsey separated them again. "Goddammit Noonan, go get the car." When Noonan was gone Dorsey turned to Zoe. "I'm sure you'll call Cooper as soon as I leave. Tell him we're coming for him."

Forty-seven

In the good old days, cab drivers got out of their taxis to help passengers with their luggage, but this was 2007. The driver dropped the passenger window and shouted across the front seat. "Hey, buddy. Trunk's open if you wanna throw your bag in."

"That's okay," Coop said. He opened the rear door and tossed the duffel onto the seat. He got in the front and sat next to the driver.

"Where to, pal?" the driver asked.

"D'ya know any car rental agencies downtown?"

"There's about a dozen of them right here in the terminal."

"Yeah, I know, but I have to get downtown right away...a business thing."

The driver pulled a lever and the meter rewound to five dollars and fifty cents. "Gotcha, I know a place."

Using his alias and half of what little cash he had left, Coop rented a Wrangler with four-wheel drive. He hopped onto I-95 northbound and followed the same route he took when McNamara was with him, only this time the dirt road leading to the cabin was covered with snow from an early season storm. Coop stopped, used a lever to engage four-wheel drive and plowed forward through six inches of slush.

He ran out of road and turned off the engine. Using his good arm, he grabbed the duffel and the tire iron and plodded through the snow to the cabin. The door was ajar. Apparently, McNamara had been in a hurry to get the hell out of there.

The cot was repositioned next to the stove and the wood stack was down to three logs. He disconnected the stovepipe, nudged the stove about a foot to the left and used the tire iron to pry three floorboards loose. He dropped the duffel into the opening, replaced the boards, pushed the stove back, and reconnected the pipe.

On the way back to D.C., he stopped in College Park and bought a burner phone that would work in the U.S. He called Zoe. "How'd it go?" he asked.

"Fine, but I thought Noonan would have a shit-hemorrhage."

Coop laughed. "Was Dorsey with him?"

"Yeah, he told me to tell you he's coming for you."

"It figures. He's had his eye on my office for the last year."

"The offer's still open to stay at my place," Zoe said.

"I appreciate it, but I'll get a motel room."

"Okay, but call me when you get settled...and Coop..."

"Yeah."

"Call the doctor."

Coop checked his nest egg; it was under five hundred dollars. When he got near D.C., he stopped at a Dollar Store and bought a pair of khakis, a shirt, and fresh socks; then he cruised through a low-end motel district and found a room for $240 a week. It wasn't quite a Motel six, but it wasn't a four either. The sheets were clean and the plumbing worked, so it would do. After a twenty-minute shower, he called Josh. "Hey, buddy. It's me."

Josh was sitting on the couch with Rusty's head in his lap. "Hi Dad, I knew you were home."

"Really? How did you know?"

"Your friend told me."

"Oh yeah? Which friend is that?

"He didn't say his name, but he said he worked with you."

"Where did you run into him?"

"He was parked in front of our house when I got the morning paper."

"Really. Did he say anything else?"

"Just that it was too bad you missed my game last night."

"Listen, Josh, I don't want you talking to people you don't know. Sometimes they're not really friends."

"Oh, okay."

"Good. Put Mom on, will ya?"

"Sure, hold on."

Josh carried the phone to the kitchen and handed it to Fran. "You're back?" she asked.

"Yeah, this morning. Listen, some strange guy's been following Josh around. Maybe you should keep him around the house today."

"Okay, but I'm sure it's no coincidence that this guy shows up the same day you do. Are you in some kind of trouble?"

"I dunno, maybe. Look, I'm coming over to pick up a few things. I'll fill you in then." Before Coop left the motel, he ran through a mental list of Agency people he thought he could trust. Other than Zoe, it was a pretty short list.

Coop parked in the driveway of what used to be his home and looked up and down the street. It was empty. A hollow pit formed in his stomach as he climbed the stairs to the front porch. He started to put his key in the lock before having second thoughts. He rang the doorbell. Josh opened the door and threw his arms around Coop's waist. Coop cradled Josh's head against his chest.

Coop looked up and saw Fran standing in the doorway. "I'm glad you're back," she said.

Josh looked back and forth between his mom and dad. Fran stepped onto the porch and gave Coop a peck—well short of a kiss—on the cheek. "Really glad for Josh."

A black sedan turned the nearby corner and screeched to a stop in front of the house. Before Dorsey could even shut off the engine, Noonan hopped out and was swaggering toward the porch. He forced himself in front of Fran and Josh as if they didn't exist and grabbed Coop by the arm. "The man wants to talk to you."

Coop broke loose of Noonan's grip. "Tell him I'll come by later."

"That won't do, asshole."

"Watch your mouth," Coop said. He shoved Noonan backward and he stumbled down the stairs, landing on his butt.

Noonan came charging back up the steps, but by then Dorsey had joined the scene and restrained him. "Coop, he wants to see you now. Let's not have a scene in front of your family," Dorsey said.

Fran looked at Coop. "What's going on?"

He nudged Fran toward the door. "I'll tell you later. Take Josh inside and don't open the door for anyone. I'll be back as soon as I can."

Dorsey handed the keys to Noonan, "You drive, we'll ride in the back."

Once they were on their way, Dorsey said, "Empty your pockets." Coop handed him his wallet, passport, a ring of keys and a single key with a diamond-shaped tag that had the number 27 printed on it. Dorsey held it up. "Where's the motel?"

"Why? Looking for a place to bring your girlfriend?"

Dorsey held his temper. "Look, I'm trying to make this easy on you."

"Okay, it's on Arlington Boulevard," Coop said.

It didn't take long for Dorsey and Noonan to search the room, but Noonan wasn't satisfied. He kept throwing stuff around, making sure he left as big a mess as possible. "Where's the duffel?" Noonan said.

"I'll give you a hint. It's not here," Coop said. He looked at Dorsey. "How can you work with this idiot, anyway?" Noonan's face turned crimson.

"Let's go see Randy," Dorsey said.

~ * ~

Randy was pacing back and forth with a glass of liquor in his hand when Dorsey and Noonan opened the door and shoved Coop into his office. Randy showed a smug expression. "Thanks, guys, give us some privacy, will ya?" The two agents left the room. Randy turned to Coop. "Drink?"

"No, just get on with it," Coop said.

Randy gulped the remainder of his drink and set the glass on a table. "Okay, I want my money."

"Your money?"

"Yeah, my money."

"Isn't it the Agency's money?"

"Fuck the Agency. I worked for that dough. I earned it. It's mine."

Coop gave a mocking laugh. "Earned it? What a joke. I guess piling up bodies pays well these days."

"Don't start with your moral high ground crap. You're the one who killed all those people on the island."

"At least it wasn't to line my pockets. You...you sonofabitch... shot me in the back just to keep your corrupt scheme a secret. It's kind of ironic though, isn't it?"

"What is?"

"This situation. After all of your double-dealing and double-crossing, I have the money and you don't."

"Look, I never planned to shoot you. I told you not to come to that meeting. But, no, you had to be the boy scout and show up anyway."

"Oh, I get it. It was my fault you shot me. Well, how's this for being a boy scout? How about instead of giving you the money, I tell the director everything and you spend the next twenty years in jail?"

Randy snickered. "Tell him what?"

"Tell him there never was any gold and you knew it...and tell him you found the Yellowcake and sold it to Iran to make nuclear fuel, and how about the hi-jacking of Burma five-seven-one to..."

Randy interrupted. "Man, you're as naïve as ever. Who'd believe you? An old burned-out agent who spends three hours a week on a psychiatrist's couch. And where's the proof? Everything went up in smoke when you set fire to that island: the airplane, the Yellowcake, the nuclear plant, everything."

"Everything except the money, and you know what? I'll burn that too before I let you get your hands on it."

The deputy director pointed his finger at Coop. "Listen pal, don't underestimate me. One way or another, I'll get that money."

"You think I'm scared of you? What the hell could you do to an old burned-out agent like me?"

"A lot more than you could imagine. You've got twenty-four hours. If I don't have it by then..."

"Then what?"

"Then I'll come for it. And you know I'm not one to be concerned with collateral damage."

"Collateral damage? What's that supposed to mean?"

"You figure it out. By the way, it's too bad Josh didn't have anyone at his game the other night. What with you gone and Fran pulling a double shift at the hospital, there was nobody to keep an eye him."

Coop clenched his teeth so hard his cheek muscles bulged. He threw a left hook that caught Randy under the right eye, knocking him down on one knee. He lunged, forcing Randy flat on his back. When Randy tried to get up, Coop clasped his hands around his neck and started to squeeze.

Dorsey and Noonan heard the commotion and barged through the door. They pounced on Coop and dragged him off Randy. Randy rose to his feet, coughing and rubbing his neck. He glared at Coop who was still being restrained by the two agents and he buried his fist into Coop's gut. Coop doubled over. "It's personal now," Randy said. He delivered another blow above the solar plexus. This time Coop heard a cracking sound and he vomited on Randy's rug.

Forty-eight

Fran sent Josh to his room to do homework, while she stared out the window and waited; it had been almost three hours since Coop had been whisked away in the back seat of the Agency car.

A familiar-looking black sedan screeched around the corner and pulled to the curb in front of the house. The rear door flung open and Coop tumbled out. The car sped off, leaving him lying in the gutter next to the sidewalk. Fran bolted down the stairs and rushed to his side. "Coop, are you okay?"

Coop tried to get to his knees, but he couldn't make it. He groaned and fell backwards. "I'll be okay, just help me inside."

Fran placed Coop's arm over her shoulder and they slowly walked to the house. Once inside, she sat him down in the kitchen. This wasn't the first broken rib Fran had treated. She filled a plastic bag with ice and had Coop hold it against his ribcage while she rounded up Ace bandages and several rolls of adhesive tape. Coop winced as the bandages were cinched around his midsection. "Too tight?" Fran asked.

"No, it's fine."

She secured the bandages with several strips of tape and leaned back to admire her handiwork. "Don't sneeze or cough or you'll regret it." She pulled up a chair and sat next to him. "So, did you find the guy who shot you?"

Coop closed his eyes for a moment and replayed that December night in Sadr City. "Yeah, I found him."

"How do you feel about it now?

He grimaced as he let out a breath. "Betrayed," he said. "I feel betrayed."

"So, was it worth trading your marriage for?"

"Is that what I did?" Coop said. Fran didn't answer. "Is that really what I did?"

A tear rolled down Fran's cheek. "Coop, I still love you, but I can't take it anymore. Look, look at us right now. You've had the crap beaten out of you, we're afraid to let Josh out of the house and I...I have no idea what's going on."

Coop touched Fran's hand. "I'm so sorry. You were right. I should have let this whole thing go when you told me to." He shifted in the chair and grimaced. "Oh, man, that hurts. Are there any of those Oxycontins left over from my operation?"

"There's a half a bottle."

"Get me one, will ya? Then I'll tell you everything that's been going on."

Fran gave Coop the tablet along with a swig of water. He eased back in the chair and let everything out: the missing gold, the missing plane, the missing island, the Yellowcake, the duffel full of money, Randy's betrayal, and today's scene in his office.

"So, you're going to give him the money. Right?"

"I dunno. I have to think about it."

"What's to think about? Give him the damn money and you'll be done with it."

"It's not that easy. I know everything this man did and he knows I know. I'm not sure it will be over until he kills me. Yeah, I gotta think about it." He pressed his hands against the dressing to put pressure on his side as he tried to stand. It felt like Randy's punch all over again. He flopped back in the chair.

"That's it, you're staying here tonight. I'll make up the bed in the extra room," Fran said.

"You sure?"

"I'm sure, but don't think everything is all right between us."

Coop made his way up the stairs to the extra bedroom. He had convinced Fran to give him another Oxy and when the second pill kicked in, he fell into a deep sleep. He woke with a start; a whining sound was coming from the hallway. He looked at the clock. It was 2:35 a.m. Coop hugged his midsection, rolled out of bed and made his way to open the door. Rusty was sitting on his hind legs, his tail wagging. "Okay, boy. I'll let you out."

He shuffled down the stairs with the golden retriever close behind and opened the door to the back yard. Rusty stuck his nose out, but wouldn't go any further, and from deep down in his gut he emitted a low-pitched growl. Coop looked into the yard. "What's up, buddy?" Rusty lifted his snout and barked twice.

Coop took a flashlight from the nearby shelf and gave Rusty a nudge. The retriever followed him outside, but stubbornly sat down and returned to growl mode. Coop swept the beam across the grass and then against a cedar fence. Rusty took off barking and jumped against the slats. Coop moved closer to the fence and focused his light across the top. Two eyes were staring down at him. A loud meow followed and a cat scrambled across the top of the fence. Rusty ran alongside but gave up when the feline disappeared into the neighbor's yard. Coop turned off the flashlight. "You crazy dog. I'm going back to bed." It took a while to climb the stairs and when he eventually made it to the top and laid down on the bed, he heard Rusty start barking all over again.

The opioids were still circulating in Coop's bloodstream and it didn't take long for him to pass out. He slept soundly for a couple of hours before he was startled awake by a gut-wrenching sound. It was coming from the backyard.

Coop forgot about his ribs and jumped out of bed. The pain hit him like an electric cattle prod; he groaned and reached for the bandage. His pistol was in the dresser drawer. He grabbed it and checked the magazine for ammunition on his way to the back door.

He rushed into the yard and did a sweep with his flashlight. A chill went through his body when the beam caught sight of Rusty. He wasn't moving and his head was at an awkward angle. Ignoring his ribs, Coop sprinted to the animal. He pointed the light directly at the ground where the dog was lying. Rusty's throat had been slashed.

Forty-nine

Coop and Fran covered Rusty with a blanket and tried to restrain Josh from going into the yard, but he broke loose and raced to the dead dog. He pulled off the shroud and fell on the body hugging and kissing it. After giving Josh some time, Coop lifted him to his feet. Fran tried to talk to him, but he was unresponsive—just looking off into space. Coop dialed 911. An ambulance arrived five minutes later.

Josh was placed in a hospital room on the 4th floor and injected with 10 mg of Valium. He closed his eyes and drifted off. A doctor came in shortly, checked Josh's vitals and turned to Coop and Fran. "It's a form of post-traumatic stress disorder."

Coop was personally familiar with PTSD. "How bad?"

"It's hard to say. We'll know more when he wakes up." The doctor dimmed the lights. "He'll sleep for quite a while. There's a lounge at the end of the hall. Why don't you folks get some rest."

They were exhausted and sank into the lounge couches. "It's my fault," Coop said.

"No, it's Randy's."

"I dunno. Maybe I should have just given in to him and taken my chances."

"Your chances on being killed? No way. If you do give it to him, at least even up the odds a little."

Coop pulled himself from the couch and checked out the snack table. "Coffee?" he asked.

"Sure."

He filled two Styrofoam cups and handed one to Fran. "What now?" she asked.

"This is a tough battle to fight; Randy holds all cards. I'm thinking I'll give him the money."

"What about evening the odds?"

"I'll try to watch my back." Coop's phone buzzed and he checked the caller ID. "It's him," he said and he stepped into the hall.

"Fuck you," Coop shouted into the phone.

"Is that any way to greet an old buddy? You should be happy it was just the dog."

"Do you have any idea the damage you've done?"

"Big deal. Get him another dog."

"My son, asshole. He's doped up on medication. You put a ten-year-old in a hospital bed. Does that even bother you?"

"Not really. I've never been that fond of kids."

"You're a fuckin' sociopath."

Randy laughed into the mouthpiece. "And you're a fuckin' dead man."

"You can't kill me. I'm the only one who knows where the money is."

"You know what? I just had a wave of empathy. Maybe I'll send your kid a stuffed animal or something. Room four-nineteen. Right?" Coop didn't answer. "Hey, are you still there?" Randy said.

Coop sat down on a wheelchair parked in the hallway. "Okay, look, I just want this thing to be over with."

"Fine. Let's work it out."

"I'm listening," Coop said.

"You get early retirement along with a bonus. Then you get the hell out of D.C. and nobody in the Agency hears from you again."

Two nurses passed by. They looked at Coop sitting in the wheelchair and gave him a disapproving look. He waved and waited until they were out of earshot.

"How about Zoe?"

"What's she got to do with this?"

"I want her to come out of this okay."

"What? You banging her or something?"

"You are a prick. Maybe if you'd ever had a friend..."

"Okay, I'll throw her a promotion. I'll make her part of my personal team."

"How do I know you'll actually do it?"

Randy laughed. "You don't. I guess you'll just have to trust me."

"Trust you? Are you fuckin' kidding me?"

"Let's face it, man. You don't have a choice."

Coop was going to tee off again on Randy, but instead he took inventory of his injuries: a black eye, a bruised shoulder, and a broken rib. He sighed. "Okay, how do we seal the deal?"

"You drop the duffel at my office and I hand you your check and your retirement papers."

Coop shook his head and laughed. "Your office? Why is my trust meter registering zero again?"

"A public place then. Hold on a minute." Randy tapped his computer and did a quick search. He ran through a database and brought up a street map of Washington D.C. "How...how about... let's see..." He scrolled the map. "How about the Mayflower Hotel?"

"When?" Coop asked.

"Tonight. I'll meet you out front at eleven o'clock."

"Are you bringing along muscle?"

"I'll be alone."

He suspected Randy was probably lying, but with the cancer looming, he didn't have much to lose. "Fine, eleven o'clock," Coop said.

Fifty

Since the scene in Randy's office, when Randy dressed McNamara down for defending Coop, McNamara's work environment had been made miserable. It was no secret in the Agency that when a shit-job came up, Randy would automatically assign it to McNamara and McNamara would comply. Today Randy dropped the big one, the one McNamara wasn't sure he could carry out.

McNamara's heart began to pound and his mouth felt like he'd been chewing on a ball of cotton. The Exchange Saloon, a favorite watering hole for agents, was only two blocks away. He made a beeline for it.

~ * ~

Coop asked Zoe to meet him at the Starbucks on G Street. They ordered a couple of mochas and took seats in the back of the coffee house. "Fill me in," Zoe said.

Coop took a slug of the coffee. He winced and swallowed hard. "Jeez, that's hot."

Zoe laughed. "Live with it. Come on, what's going on?"

He gulped down a healthy dose of ice water. "I made a deal with Randy. He gets the money; I get early retirement."

"That's it?"

"You get a spot on his personal team."

Zoe spit out her coffee. "I'm not working with that bastard."

"Hey, you're only forty-three years old. You can suck it up for another twelve years."

"No way. Not with that asshole."

"Look, you don't have to go out for drinks with the guy, just do your job."

"I'm not going to do it."

"Okay, that's up to you, but it's part of the deal if you change your mind."

"Sorry, I don't trust him."

"I don't either, but it's the best I could do."

"We need to come up with a plan B."

"Yeah, well let me know if you get one, but as it stands, I'm meeting Randy in front of the Mayflower Hotel at eleven p.m." He picked a napkin from the table, took a pen from his pocket and drew a crude map. "Do you have four-wheel drive on that Toyota?"

"Yeah, why?"

"I need you to pick up the duffel for me." He slid the map in front of Zoe. "This is the way to the hunting shack. Just push the stove to the side and pry up the floorboard."

Zoe looked at the map. "No problem, it's only a couple hours' round trip. I'll head out there right away."

"Thanks. I'll be waiting a block south of the Mayflower on L Street. Make sure to get it to me by ten-fifteen at the latest."

"No problem. I'll be there well before ten, but do you have any insurance against a Randy double-cross?"

Coop shook his head. "I'll be on my own."

"I'm coming with you."

"No, that's not going to happen. I almost got you killed in Iraq and it didn't feel very good. I'm handling this alone."

"But..."

Coop pushed back his chair and came to Zoe. He hugged her as hard as his ribs would allow. "Zoe, other than Fran and Josh, I love you more than anyone in this world...so I'm handling this alone. That's an order and I don't want to hear any more about it."

She kissed him on the cheek. "I love you too, Coop. Be careful, please."

After leaving Starbucks, Zoe headed uptown to her apartment on G Street. A couple of blocks ahead she spotted the colorful sign of the Exchange Saloon. It crossed her mind to stop in and see if anyone from the Agency was hanging around, but it was just a few minutes after two—a little early even for spies.

As she passed the entrance to the bar, a guy who was paying little attention to where he was going walked right into her and knocked her on her butt. The man leaned down to help. "Sorry, so sorry, I guess I was daydreaming," he said.

Zoe reached for his extended hand. "Mac?"

McNamara looked surprised. "Zoe?" He helped her to her feet and pointed to the door. "Were you headed to the Saloon?"

"No, I just left a meeting with Coop."

The sound of Coop's name caused the smile to disappear from McNamara's face. "Hey, what the hell did you guys find over there in Iraq anyway?"

"What do you mean?"

"Randy is fuming and bad-mouthing Coop. He's been on my case, too."

"Look, Mac, you know I can't talk about an assignment until the report is released."

"Yeah, I know, but I was hoping you could make an exception."

Zoe tilted her head. "Why? You're not involved in this op."

"It looks like I'm getting involved." He motioned toward the saloon door. "Let's have a beer. Just tell me whatever you can."

"I don't know…"

"Please, one beer. I'll buy."

She checked the time. "Okay, sure. I've got a couple of minutes."

Two hours later, Zoe left the Exchange Saloon and walked another block uptown. The street was noisy, but up ahead she spotted an office building with a large foyer. She went inside and found a quiet spot in the corner. She took out her phone, tapped in the country code for Zurich, Switzerland and followed it with a ten-digit number.

Fifty-one

Coop found a spot near the hospital entrance, took a Baskin-Robbins bag from the front seat and walked toward the elevators. He ran the logistics of tonight's meeting through his brain one more time. When the elevator doors opened, his mind was somewhere else and he bumped smack into a man who was on his way out. "Excuse me, so sorry," Coop said.

The man did a double take. "Mr. Cooper?"

He looked up. "Oh, Dr. Goodman. Sorry, I almost knocked you over."

"No problem, I'm glad I bumped into you." He laughed. "I didn't mean literally bumped into you, but I was going to call you. I was hoping we could start your treatments."

"Yeah, I was meaning to get in touch. Listen, if things go well for me, I'll start in a day or two. If they don't...well, I might not need any treatments."

Dr. Goodman looked confused. "Why would you not need treatments?"

"It's complicated, Doc. Hopefully, I'll call you in a couple of days."

Coop opened the door to Josh's room and peeked inside. Josh was sitting up in bed, playing Go Fish with Fran. He looked a lot better than he had in the morning. "How're you feeling?" Coop asked.

Josh scooped up two aces and took his eyes off his cards. "Good. Really good."

"That's great. Who's winning?"

"I am, but I don't think Mom's trying too hard."

"I am too," Fran said.

Coop laughed and handed Josh a plastic cup with a big red, white and blue straw poking from the top. "Chocolate. Save me a sip, will ya?"

Josh sucked up a mouthful of the melted ice cream. "Thanks, Dad."

Coop glanced at Fran and then toward the door. "Hey, Josh, will you be okay if Mom and I get a cup of coffee?"

"Sure."

They stepped into the lounge and plopped onto one of the couches. "Everything's set for tonight," Coop said.

"Did you pick up the money?" Fran asked.

"Zoe's on her way right now and she'll get it to me by ten. I'm meeting Randy at eleven."

Fran's eyes narrowed. "What assurance do you have that once you give him the money, he won't turn his goons loose on you?"

"None, but I checked out the front of the hotel and I didn't see any place where they could hide without me spotting them."

"God, be careful Coop." He tried to speak, but no words came out. "What is it?" Fran asked.

Coop gazed out the window, not really focusing on anything. "Fran, I have to know. If tonight doesn't end in disaster, is there any chance we can ever be a family again?"

Fran hesitated. "I love you, Coop, but I love our son more. He can't be worried every time you leave the house that there's a chance you'll never come back."

"Look, I'm out of the spy business. By this time tomorrow, I'll be officially retired."

"Then what? I don't see you as a stay-at-home dad cooking dinner while I'm at work."

He thought about what Fran said. He knew she was right. He was a type A and there was no way he could spend his day cleaning house and watching Oprah reruns. "I'll find something—something new," he said."

"Like what? A cop? Maybe a detective? As long as you go to work with a shoulder holster, nothing will really change."

"I'll find something else. Something with a nice desk and no shoulder holster. I know I will."

Fran wanted to believe him, but history wasn't on Coop's side. "When you deliver on that promise, we'll talk about being a family again. Right now, you have to concentrate on getting through tonight. Be careful."

Fifty-two

A person carrying a rectangular suitcase entered the third-floor office directly across the street from the Mayflower Hotel. The snaps of a leather case were popped open and the components of a telescopic rifle were removed and mounted in the street-side window.

~ * ~

Coop parked his rental car on L Street, a block south of the hotel. He looked at his watch again. It was 10:05. He lit a cigarette... and then another...and another. He checked the time again. It was 10:45 and he still hadn't heard from Zoe. He'd already left four voicemails, but he dialed her number again anyway. This time she answered. "Coop, is that you?"

"Where the hell are you? It's getting late."

"That dirt road blew a tire on me. I had to figure out how to change it and now I'm driving on that little donut spare."

"You going to make it in time?"

"Yeah, but it'll be close. Just stay on the corner of Connecticut and L and I'll pass you the duffel."

"You sure?"

"Don't worry, I won't let you down."

~ * ~

Randy arrived at the Mayflower an hour early and headed to the bar for a double scotch. He checked the clock behind the bar every few minutes until ten fifty-five, then he stepped out of the hotel and stationed himself twelve feet from the revolving glass doors. His left eye was twitching uncontrollably as he glanced up at the window across the street. He could only make out a silhouette, but he nodded anyway.

~ * ~

Coop was still a block south of the hotel waiting for Zoe. He flipped his phone open. It was 10:58. He glanced down the street; Randy was pacing back and forth in front of the hotel. Coop waited another fifteen minutes until he knew he couldn't wait any longer, then he began walking empty-handed toward the hotel entrance.

A car approached from behind and screeched to a halt right next to him. The passenger window rolled down and the duffel flew out and landed on the sidewalk right next to him. "Good luck," McNamara said.

Coop shouted back at him. "What the...where's Zoe?" The car sped off. Coop didn't have time to think about it. He hoisted the duffel over his good shoulder and hastened his step.

The shooter spied Coop a half a block away and swiveled the rifle, putting him directly in the crosshairs as he approached the hotel entrance. Through the sight, the shooter had a closeup view of the confrontation between Coop and Randy.

Randy looked angry. "You're late."

Coop ignored the greeting. "I'm here now," he said, performing a three-sixty scan of the area. "You alone?"

"I said I would be."

Randy's words weren't convincing enough for Coop. He spotted two guys exiting the hotel by way of the revolving glass door. From his vantage point they looked a lot like Dorsey and Noonan. Coop set down the duffel and reached for his Glock.

"What the fuck are you doing?" Randy said.

The two men staggered onto the sidewalk and turned toward them. They both looked about twenty-one years old and both were drunk as skunks. They wobbled off down the street.

"Nothing. Just playing it safe. That's all," Coop said.

"Well, put your weapon away. I told you I'd be here alone."

Coop studied the surroundings again. The street was empty except for the two drunks who by now were almost a block away. He put his Glock back in the holster and nudged the duffel in Randy's direction. "A lot of blood spilled because of this."

"If you don't mind, I'll take the money without the lecture." Randy unzipped the case. His eyes narrowed to slits. "What the hell?"

Coop stared at the open duffel; wadded-up newspapers spilled from the top of the case. He bent down and pulled several bricks and the Sunday comics out of the satchel. The cash was gone.

"Is this your idea of a joke?" Randy said.

Coop's mind was racing.

Randy realized he wasn't getting his big payoff tonight. He looked up at the office window and raised his hand to stop the process he had set in motion. He was too late. A muzzle flash lit up the window and the gunshot echoed through the still midnight air.

Fifty-three

Arlington Cemetery. Two Weeks Later

Rows of cars lined the road near the gravesite and others spilled out onto adjacent streets. Several dozen people, most dressed in black, surrounded the coffin that was poised for burial. The majority of the mourners were Agency people paying respect to a fallen comrade-in-arms.

McNamara didn't want to join the crowd. Instead, he held back and leaned against the trunk of an old maple. He caught part of the minister's eulogy, "...and he was taken in the prime of his life by a terrorist's bullet." He walked away.

Twenty minutes later, he climbed the stairs to the government building that housed the deputy director's office. The flag was at half-staff. He paused in front of it for a moment before going through the security screening.

McNamara entered the empty reception room and knocked on the deputy director's private office door. A voice from inside said, "Come on in."

The deputy director was sitting in his swivel chair, looking out the window and chewing a wad of gum. "Where have you been? he asked.

"Sorry, boss, but I felt the least I could do was pay my respects."

"I guess you're right, but I couldn't bring myself to do it." The deputy director rotated his chair. His sandy-gray hair was gone and the top of his bald head glistened.

"How's the chemo going?" McNamara asked.

"Good, it's goin' good. So, any idea where Zoe is?"

"Face it, Coop, she's gone." McNamara handed him an envelope. "She told me to give you this after things settled down."

"She did? When?"

"When we swapped assignments."

"Why didn't you tell me?"

"She told me not to. She said 'just give Coop this envelope. He'll understand.'" He started for the door. "By the way, thanks for the promotion. It almost makes up for my earlobe."

Coop showed a sheepish grin. "Yeah, sorry about that. I'm going to make it up to you?"

"I was kidding. You already have?"

"I don't mean for the ear. I'm talking about what you and Zoe did for me. I owe you both."

"You don't owe me; it was all Zoe. She called it her plan B. Hang in there, boss."

Coop watched the door close behind McNamara and then looked down at the envelope he had delivered. He held it up to the light and could see it didn't hold a letter, so he slit it open and gave it a good shake. A postcard fell into his lap. He recognized it right away. It had a picture of the ocean and a girl in a bikini along with the caption: HAVING FUN IN THE COCOS.

The words scribbled on the back, written in red ink, were his own: *Craig Cooper owes Zoe Fields $8,800.* Below in black ink, in the same handwriting as the envelope, was written: *Coop, let's call it even. Thanks for the advice. I wanted it bad enough and I found a way to make it happen. Love you. Z.*

Coop smiled and tossed the card into the trash.

Meet Mike Paull

Mike Paull, a native of the San Francisco Bay Area, had two passions that preceded his writing career. He is a licensed dentist and a licensed commercial pilot. In 2000, he retired from dental practice and devoted his time to recreational flying. In 2010, he retired from flying and embarked on his new career—writing.

Mike's first book, Tales from the Sky Kitchen Café, is a series of short stories describing his experiences as a pilot hanging out in a small airport coffee shop. His next series of books, the Brett Raven Mystery Trilogy, features a dentist as the protagonist and mystery solver. Missing, a spy thriller, is Mike's newest creation.

Mike and his wife Bev now live two hundred miles north of San Francisco in Chico, CA.

Letter to Our Readers

Enjoy this book?

You can make a difference

As an independent publisher, Wings ePress, Inc. does not have the financial clout of the large New York Publishers. We can't afford large magazine spreads or subway posters to tell people about our quality books.

But, we do have something much more effective and powerful than ads. We have a large base of loyal readers.

Honest Reviews help bring the attention of new readers to our books.

If you enjoyed this book, we would appreciate it if you would spend a few minutes posting a review on the site where you purchased this book or on the Wings ePress, Inc. webpages at:
https://wingsepress.com/

Visit Our Website

For The Full Inventory

Of Quality Books:

Wings ePress.Inc
https://wingsepress.com/

Quality trade paperbacks and downloads
in multiple formats,
in genres ranging from light romantic comedy
to general fiction and horror.
Wings has something for every reader's taste.
Visit the website, then bookmark it.
We add new titles each month!

Wings ePress Inc.

3000 N. Rock Road

Newton, KS 67114